SEEDS OF SILENCE

SEEDS OF SILENCE

Mercedes Salisachs

Translation by Gretta K. Siebentritt

Jorge Pinto Books Inc.
New York

In memory of my husband,
who was an unforgettable grandfather.

M.S.

And so I emerge now from its waters dazed and confused,
  not knowing where to look, which way to go,
  licking this profuse collection of wounds
that throb in the raw core of my heart and soul.

FERNANDO SÁNCHEZ DRAGÓ

From: *La del alba sería*

I

If Gregorio had not called from Thailand barely an hour ago, I would have gone on believing that my intent to obliterate the past would eventually succeed, without too much effort and with utter impunity.

For six years, I have been telling myself that certain deaths can deliver us from the perils of traveling through life with the caution of a minesweeper, even though the memories insist on moving in and breeding in every corner, in every fluid, of our surroundings.

But it is abundantly clear that it is much harder to obliterate the past than to prevent future mistakes. I am even beginning to think that the past not only resists dying no matter how hard we try to kill it, with the passage of time it burrows in the soul like a barbed hook, which cannot be extracted without causing tears.

It hit me as soon as I replaced the receiver. Everything I believed had sunk—for better or for worse—into the muck-filled swamp that memory can become, suddenly exploded onto the surface. And I understood with utter clarity that the past does not know how to die.

To the contrary, the deaths that shook us so terribly during the course of our existence were as alive as ever.

Like it or not, the past always returns to reproach and rattle us, make demands, impose conditions, and otherwise maltreat us. It ratchets up the pain instead of relieving it.

There is nothing more eloquent than the pain we once thought easily subdued. Because some pain can never be subdued, or immobilized, or overcome. It is far too clever and slippery for us to pin it down and lock it away in the dungeons of oblivion.

Any time we look over our shoulders, then, we are liable to relive it. And Gregorio's telephone call has been just that: an unfortunate introspection, a painful examination of conscience. And all because of an unexpected "about face."

It does not help to cull from memory the short bursts of happiness we also experienced, and which left us grief-stricken when they slipped from our grasp. The painful parts always prevail, traipsing over our will and insinuating themselves comfortably into things we later look back on as the true source of our contentment.

Now I wonder how Paula will react when I tell her about the call from my son, Gregorio. Most likely Paula will not be pleased at the prospect of a child as young as my grandson Miguel invading our life.

While singularly unendowed with any great capacity for reflection or profound thought, Paula Civanco possesses an exceptional amount of the intelligence substitute popularly known as intuition. In awkward situations, she is saved by her instincts.

Therefore, when I tell her Gregorio has called me from Thailand and asked me to take charge of little Miguel, in all likelihood she will merely shrug and switch on her most seductive smile. "That sounds fine to me, Patricio. We will do whatever you say." Naturally, she will do everything in her power to put up with the child and pretend his presence at Mas Delfín for the entire summer is the best thing that could ever have happened to us.

Despite her many flaws, I have to admit that Paula is an accommodating woman. She makes few demands and does not complain when I demand more of her than she is able to give. Her sole aim, even at the risk of forfeiting her dignity as a woman, is to make sure the flame she kindled in me that summer with her seductive arts and the remarkable elasticity of her anatomy continues to blaze, even if only on the surface. Make sure her status as "eternal love of a famous writer" is not struck down by her own insipidity.

This is why she never contradicts me. Whenever she is tempted to stand up to me, she quickly takes herself in hand and becomes exceedingly submissive, bowing to the dictates of her docile, under-exercised mind.

The truth is, when I met Paula, my grandson Miguel did not even exist and there was no indication whatsoever that he might actually come into being one day. Gregorio and Dula had been married for four years with no sign of a child.

That summer had to transpire before the wound of childlessness would heal upon the couple's return to Thailand.

When I think back now on the way in which those three long months unfolded, I can see that none of what happened could be considered normal. It made no sense for Gregorio to be jealous of Rodolfo Liaño or for Paula to hold fast to me without having the faintest idea why I clung to her so tenaciously. And of course, there was the sudden eruption of fear over the possibility that flowers could speak.

It also was not normal that the summer months gave no inkling that autumn would bring anything more than shorter days and innocuous portents of winter's chill.

Before that summer, as the spring had begun to recede, everything at Mas Delfín had seemed as usual, unruffled and benign. The beach was the same as always, private and small, partly concealed by the looming bluffs, like two giant arms trying to enfold what resembled a lagoon more than open sea.

The forest was still the same jungle—virgin of memories—where the humidity caused ferns to grow in riotous abundance in a half-hidden hollow, as if to provide cover for sprites or alien beings.

And the dark crags rising up in the middle of the bay—perhaps placed there by nature so that I, upon awakening, could contemplate them from the balcony of my bedroom—were still the same unfailing sentries for far-off boats ignorant of the perils of those reefs.

That summer had to happen in order for everything at Mas Delfín to be transformed.

The truth is, the beach is no longer the same solitary lagoon, the forest no longer resembles a wild refuge for mythological creatures, and the two blackened crags are no longer a reliable beacon for unwitting sailors. And worse yet, the seagulls have deserted. One almost never hears the screeching that Dula used to describe as "moans." And when they fly towards the crags they rarely land as they used to.

Everything else at Mas Delfín continues in the same mode, except what Rodolfo Liaño once called a Wagnerian opera of pure splendor is now just a cheap imitation of a lost paradise. A hidden cove dispossessed of its wild nature.

It was not that way before. Then, the cove was still untamed, as if by some telluric whim the distant presents of long ago had been transplanted there.

"It's as if a bygone era had simply gone to sleep, only to awake on the beach of Mas Delfín," Rodolfo would say.

When something makes an impression on Rodolfo, he never fails to describe it with a certain grandiloquence. He is extraordinarily perceptive. Our conversations always yield an endless supply of literary images or unusual expressions, which I do not hesitate to insert in my books. "You'll have to pay me royalties," he jokes. "I told you that one."

In reality, Rodolfo is not just my secretary, my manager, and my agent. He is also my friend and has been since childhood. But ours is not one of those run-of-the-mill friendships that fade away or collapse out of sheer boredom. Rodolfo Liaño has never given me a chance to tire of him. He never yields to the temptation to pester, harp, or issue ultimatums. He is simply there. And he knows as well as I do that we are both willing to help the other out, but never to put the other out.

When he closed his law practice and I—after losing Juliana—decided to leave medicine to become a writer, we decided the best thing to do would be to install ourselves at Mas Delfín. We would have no commitments other than our respective professional obligations and we would be absolutely free to live our lives as we saw fit, without any explanation to anyone.

"Don't you know what it means to live in a terrestrial paradise with no snakes or forbidden fruits?" he would ask when he sensed my concern at seeing him so overworked. "Besides, anyone would be willing to work with you, Patricio. You are a national celebrity now, don't forget."

He said it teasingly, with just enough sarcasm to avoid coming across as impertinent, but I knew a genuine loyalty lay underneath those half-jokes.

He is also grateful. "I'll never forget how you saved my father's life when he was so ill," he has often said. It's his way of letting me know he will always consider himself in my debt, come what may.

Rodolfo Liaño is no longer young. Neither of us is. We therefore never make the mistake of letting ourselves be distracted by the restless pursuits of youth.

We've both acquired the maturity of those who have discovered that intentional solitude is a thousand times more desirable than imposed company. Living alone is not synonymous with disengaging from the world. The city is relatively close to the coast and there is nothing to stop Rodolfo from occasionally disappearing from Mas Delfín when work is slow.

The truth is, we share an enviable bond of friendship that enables us to communicate by simply exchanging a glance, with no need to resort to words. Then there are the long nights of conversation when the words just take over. And because of this I have learned that true friendship consists of being quiet when words are just an excuse to break the silence, and speaking when the ideas are spilling out of our maws.

Juliana also loved Rodolfo Liaño. "Don't lose him no matter what, Patricio," she often told me. Juliana did not make mistakes. She was unfailingly judicious and level-headed. To her the most important thing was for harmony to prevail in our lives.

Juliana was close to perfect. She understood, encouraged, and collaborated, while rejecting outright anything that might jeopardize our marriage and our mutual understanding.

Juliana was actually the great benefactor of Mas Delfín. The farmstead probably would never have become what it did without the gentle ministrations of her hands and her unusual projects.

It's as if I'm seeing her on the beach, half-tumbled onto the sand, her beauty still palpable, her gaze forthright. She had a unique way of surveying the landscape around her as if she wanted to absorb it all before death could absorb her. "I sometimes have the impression that this beach is an oversight of nature," she used to say.

The beach truly was a tranquil place then. It was an aquatic tongue hidden among the crags, difficult to detect from the sea. "If only we could live here year-round."

Gregorio was still a boy then and I was practicing medicine in the city, so we were only able to enjoy Mas Delfín during the summer months. "Maybe some day, when our son is grown up."

But the son had grown up and by then, his mother was gone. The only thing left was everything she had created and tended during her lifetime, and left behind as her legacy.

The first thing I noticed when I met her was her voice, muted, soft, silky. "Tell me, Juliana, who taught you how to modulate your voice." But she was not given to flattery and quickly cut me short. "I learned it from you Patricio. I couldn't possibly have failed to notice your grimaces whenever anyone spoke in a high-pitched whine.

And she would immediately change the subject.

She sometimes worried about my dedication to medicine. "You should take more vacations. You're killing yourself." But she would quickly add, "That's why I fell in love with you. I wouldn't have wanted to marry one of those so-much-an-hour and if-I-ever-saw-you before-I-don't-remember, doctors."

Another one of her important qualities was her ability to close her eyes against whatever might jeopardize our family stability. To her, everything was—or at least appeared—easy. There were never any "down sides" and any offense could be remedied. "A bad grape just needs a little sugar," she would joke.

I remember overhearing her once as she chatted with friends on the terrace at Mas Delfín. They were talking about me and from what I could gather, I was not holding up very well. Her reaction was swift: "Life is full of false truths. I refuse to believe what you are insinuating to me."

She turned suddenly towards Daní mountain and, indicating it with outstretched arm, she said, "Do you see that mountain? It is very difficult to climb to the top. It takes a lot of time and energy to scale it and reach the hermitage. But once you're up there, you can see all you've left behind as if in miniature: village, sea, roads and forests. From there one can easily see how, when it comes down to it, everything seems trivial, like little toys, and the only thing that matters is having reached the peak. This is what has happened to me. I have reached it by marrying Patricio. So, the more you try to malign him, the more you're only maligning yourselves."

I realized then that Juliana was not unaware of certain "secrets" in my life. Stupid affairs with women too smart not to realize that Doctor Gallardo was not looking for love but rather meaningless thrills to massage his male vanity and, for that matter, he had no intention of tripping over the same stone twice.

It would have been unthinkable to stray again. I was stopped dead by the fear of losing her.

Later, when she fell ill, fear even managed to cure me of my idiotic fervors with their aftertaste of an apple treated with pesticides. That was when I was the closest to her. In fact, nothing binds us more, or brings us closer to our loved ones, than the compulsory battle waged against elements that threaten to destroy our hopes.

The most important thing was to get home, to sit beside her and discuss the endless inventory of matters which, should they not be resolved soon, would be left suspended in space for all time.

"Promise me you won't waste your talent as a writer," she would repeat. And yet she had to die in order for the talent she had glimpsed to gel.

Afterward, yes. Afterward, everything she had predicted came to pass. But so did the worry of finding myself alone with my son, realizing we increasingly resembled two sleep-walkers pacing the apartment in the old section with no motivation other than to remember her.

The entire city was plunged into gloom without Juliana. Time was slipping away quickly and monotonously, like rivers that flow noiselessly towards the sea with no bends, or waterfalls, or changing currents to enliven them.

My life shambled on without a ripple, as if the nights and days were always a little behind, the skies always gray, and the aromas smothered by a contaminated fog that reeked of a city bereft of light.

So, with my son's assent, I sold the apartment and relocated permanently to Mas Delfín.

I admit the change was not easy at first. It took all my strength to oversee and keep up everything Juliana had built, furnished, and decorated.

And to remember her, especially whenever I went into the greenhouse. Juliana's presence was tangible there. The same thing happened to Canuto, the groundskeeper. "I cannot come in here without seeing the missus."

There was no doubt in Juliana's mind that flowers have souls. And naturally, she was convinced they could clearly discern human intentions, feelings, and reactions. "I'm sure they know me, Patricio. You might not think so, but plants can distinguish people's voices, scents, and behaviors."

So convinced was she of this entelechy, I felt it would have been cruel to contradict her, to demonstrate to her that plants do not have souls, not even mortal ones. If they bloom and grow and die it is because everything on earth adheres to the system established by time.

In any case, I doubt Juliana would have heeded my skepticism. Her practically insane relationship with flowers was too deeply rooted.

Her floral fanaticism was so acute she had actually outfitted the place with a sofa, chairs, and tables so the plants would feel "at home."

My God, how many times did the two of us sit there listening to music—she said music was essential to cure the plants' ailments—while Canuto made sure the stems were free of insects and the roots sufficiently moist.

I remember her showing me a yellow rose once. "Just look at her, Patricio. She's withering because her companions have died. I think she's dying too, of loneliness." And she stroked the stem, murmuring into the petals to console it.

The only living being prohibited from setting foot in the enclave was Brutus, the dog that disappeared shortly before Gregorio and Dula arrived from Thailand. But Brutus was still with us then and whenever we went into the greenhouse, he always remained by the door. "Animals have no respect for plants," she insisted.

Actually, all of this struck me as a delicious foolishness, although I have to admit, after Juliana died I started to feel unsure about things that she had never doubted.

What happened was that the contents of the greenhouse—up to then vital and vigorous—began to waste away, as if a giant hand was at work to smother the inhabitants of the place.

It was almost instantaneous. It was palpable. Everything looked washed out and completely parched. To no avail did Canuto swear up and down that he was tending to the plants just as diligently as when the missus was alive. "It's as if they found out she was dead," he would say over and over.

For a few moments I believed that maybe Juliana had been right and the flowers missed Juliana's voice, Juliana's gentleness, and Juliana's care. "This place must be made as it was before," I ordered Canuto. "I want to see it again, just as she left it."

Gregorio also noticed the unexpected decline of the greenhouse. Although still very young, he responded to everything having to do with nature nearly as much as his mother had.

From the time he was a little boy, his favorite activity during the summers at Mas Delfín was to go traipsing into the woods and find all manner of bugs and other small creatures, which he later conveyed to his makeshift laboratory to study.

"Be careful, son. Those creatures are going to give you a scare one of these days." But when it came to his penchant for animals and their possible poisons, Gregorio—who always had doubts about everything and consulted his parents over and over again before deciding whether or not to do something—was very well informed and knew exactly what to do to avoid problems.

This proclivity of his led him to study medicine. "I just want to be a researcher, Dad. I don't want to follow in your footsteps. I recognize the value of what you do, but I get depressed being around sick people."

Gregorio was bright and despite his never-ending uncertainties, he was a good student. Besides, he loved me. He loved me as much as he had loved his mother. And he almost never took a step without consulting me first.

Which is why I was at such a loss when he informed me of his future trip to Thailand.

"I hate to leave you, Dad, but it's my life's dream."

I tried to dissuade him at first.

"But son, Thailand is very far away. Why Bangkok? Why don't you find someplace closer to Spain?"

But for once, Gregorio had no doubts whatsoever. He was absolutely certain about what he had to do.

"I know, Dad. Thailand is very far away. But I promise I'll always keep in touch with you. It will be just as if there were only a couple of kilometers between us." And seeing my hesitation, he added, "Don't forget, the most important snake farm in the world is in Bangkok."

So that was the reason. It was the snake farm. His lifelong passion incarnate. And I knew I had to give in. The important thing was not whether we were separated, but to make sure my son's dream was not quashed by our togetherness.

"You're right. Don't worry about me. Being alone isn't so bad. When it comes down to it, solitude is a writer's best friend."

I had no right to hold him back. His grades—always excellent—and his demonstrated passion for the work did not warrant my placing obstacles in his path. Gregorio had always been a conscientious son and had never given us any trouble. To the contrary, I had to show him how pleased I was that, based on his own merit, the Pasteur Institute had offered him an important post in its Bangkok laboratory after he finished his doctorate.

I hugged and congratulated him, promising I would visit him in Thailand someday.

In those days, Gregorio and I still went around like two good friends. Despite the physical resemblance, no one took us for father and son.

"We could pass for brothers, Dad," he'd say jokingly. "You're still too young for people to believe you have a son my age."

He even used to tease me sometimes.

"Come on, Dad, you should get married again. I'd feel much better knowing you'd found the right woman."

Gregorio often sounded like Juliana. Had she been able to communicate with me, she too would have counseled me to remarry.

"It isn't good for a man to be alone. The Bible says so."

But my response was always the same.

"I've been spoiled, son. I doubt very much I could find another woman like your mother."

That's why the considerable distance between Thailand and Spain did not matter, nor did the howls of nostalgia that sometimes kept me awake at night. We were united despite the distance. We had between us an enduring bond, solid and unbreakable. It was there no matter what happened.

When it came down to it, we were bound by a common denominator: our mutual admiration, our shared understanding, and our need to talk to each other, to leave nothing unsaid and to keep each other up to date about the vicissitudes and problems we faced.

Then there were my books. "Have you received my latest novel?" Gregorio knew how to "read." Gregorio was not the type of reader who "devoured" books. He savored them. He never lost the thread of what I was trying to say. His critiques, therefore, were always tremendously gratifying.

That was true even when Gregorio was still in the habit of expressing doubts about his problems. "You don't think I'm making a mistake, Dad? Should I go ahead with it?"

And he wouldn't relax until I said, "Trust your judgment, Gregorio. Of course you're not mistaken."

So now when I think about what happened later, it's hard for me to figure out where the breakdown was. Nothing seems to make sense. Nothing follows the rules established between Gregorio and me ever since—ten years ago now—he went to live in Bangkok.

Sometimes I think maybe one of my books could have triggered his suspicions about things I might have been unable to hide. Yet no matter how many times I go back over the vaguely "dangerous" passages from my novels, I have failed to find any slip-up.

The truth is, every time I have embarked on a new novel, I have done so on the margins of my own history and nothing I have written over the years is based on my real life.

Naturally, certain passages might contain some fragment of nostalgia or fear, of hopes or mistakes that are exclusively mine. Life is full of hidden recesses. "We're all hiding something," Rodolfo Liaño once told me. "Maybe that's why we humans sometimes feel so isolated from each other."

But bright as my son is, I doubt very much these feeble literary detours could have led to his recalcitrance.

There had been too many years of close communication—of frank confidences, mutual, and unconditional support, things that had strengthened our bonds as father and son, had assured us that, time and distance notwithstanding, we would never lose each other—to believe the solid flooring of our relationship should have collapsed just like that.

And worse yet, it all happened so quickly. There was no warning, no echo of the emptiness that awaited me, to prepare me for what was to come.

Suddenly, there was silence. A silence so drastic that at first I had trouble believing it was real. The blockade came later.

Gone were the mutual confidences, the constant communication, his voice—always warm and confiding—, and of course, the affectionate companionship that had endured without interruption for seven years, traversing space and scoffing at oceans, rivers, cities, and uncertainties.

This is how it has been between Gregorio and me for three years now. Three long years of questions and of shadows.

Until, all at once, the telephone rang.

❊   ❊   ❊

"So your son has finally shown signs of life."

As Patricio expected, Paula Civanco is there sunbathing on the beach. She is arranged on a pink towel with the air of the irresistible woman who six years ago had ignited the passions of Doctor Gallardo.

"And might one inquire as to what he had to say for himself? How does he explain his long silence?"

"He offered no explanations. He just asked me to do him a favor."

The response exasperates Paula. She turns antagonistic. It is a wishy-washy sort of antagonism which, at the first sign of impotence, quickly turns to milder means to solve its problems.

"And you probably said, 'how nice. Whatever you like. That's what a father is for.'"

She sounds uneasy, even though she is aware that the mistakes between father and son are nothing to her. If she gets annoyed, ultimately it allows Patricio Gallardo to unload the particular sadness that has gripped him since Gregorio took it upon himself to ignore his father.

"Exactly."

Paula turns onto her side, lowering her bikini strap to avoid a tan line.

"You'll do as you see fit."

At the moment, what Doctor Gallardo is doing is contemplating the woman's back and wondering how he could possibly have spent so many years with her.

It is not easy to describe Paula. Perhaps her most salient feature is the surprise factor. Everything about her is surprising. Her undeniable Barbie doll glamour, her perfectly proportioned body, the dazzling blue eyes that seem to devour rather than observe. Then there is her blonde, always windswept, mane and the poses of a professional model, at once civilized and decadent, and perfectly suited to the finer points of the wildest sex.

"And might one inquire as to what Gregorio has requested?"

He wants me to take charge of Miguel until he and his wife have gotten settled in Brazil."

All at once, Paula reacts. She rises slightly, turns towards him wide-eyed, and begins to rebuke him.

"Just like that? And he isn't capable of apologizing for how he's been behaving towards you?"

"No apology is necessary, Paula. It's enough to know my son has decided to break down the barrier between us."

Paula does not belabor the point. For what? Ultimately, nothing she could say will change a thing. For some time now, Paula has been playing the stunning but vapid woman, a role the writer assigned to her when they first met a few days before the opening of the Verde Mar hotel on the outskirts of the nearby town.

She realizes that Patricio does not listen to her. He does not even pay attention when—with the best of intentions and armed with a strong dose of courage—she ventures an opinion on one of his books.

Patricio regards Paula's literary opinions as unfailingly trite, or infantile, or devoid of any compelling principles, and inherently lacking in common sense.

"Look, Paula. Just because you are in a relationship with a writer does not mean you have to share in his literary creations as well."

Sometimes Patricio can be outright cruel to Paula. Especially when she dares to confuse what he writes with his real life.

"Do you honestly think I'm stupid enough to expose myself to being compared to my characters?"

Nor does he like it when Paula—joining him and his friends for an evening of conversation—tries to play the sophisticated woman, particularly when she presumes to know Patricio "better than anyone else" just because she is his lover.

"Get what I'm about to say into your head, Paula. You don't know me and I don't expect you ever will. If you really knew me, you would never allow yourself to dress the way you do, or speak in that exasperating tone of voice, and you wouldn't make one banal comment after another when conversing with my friends."

Although Patricio's cruelty cuts her to the quick, Paula quickly puts it out of her mind. She has been putting up with his outbursts for too long for the pain to last.

What is more, Patricio, for all that he tries to put her down, also has a way of carrying her to the loftiest heights, especially when he introduces her to everybody as his muse. . . .

Sometimes her lover's jovial wit, try as he might to disguise it with bluster, sweeps away his negative side and even manages to make Paula happy. When this happens, it's as if the six years of familiarity vanish and the two have just met for the first time.

They first saw each other at the Verde Mar hotel, shortly before its grand opening. Paula was an eighteen-year-old poured into a willowy, perfectly formed body and she was adept at using her eyes to confound all other glances. There was a reason the hotel management had hired her to work in public relations.

"Never have I seen such a dazzling vision," Patricio commented to Rodolfo Liaño.

It was a raucous evening during which the alcohol, pounding music, and burning hot atmosphere—replete with all sorts of sappy foolishness—contributed greatly to confusing sensation with sentiment.

Human beings, thinking they are opening the door to paradise, frequently find themselves falling into an abyss.

It was totally ridiculous, but everything conspired to make the impression caused by the very young Paula, with her brazen look and striking figure, the highlight of Patricio's evening.

What followed was an unexpected confluence of circumstances that was impossible to prevent.

Patricio dreamed about her that night. He imagined her to be as intelligent as she was beautiful, as tactful as she was attractive. For her part, Paula was certain Patricio was the love of her life. She would never love another man the way she found herself loving him.

In any event, one thing was left very clear between them from the start of their impetuous romance. "No ties. No living together. No giving up our freedom."

Even the most excessive ardor frequently gives way to moments of lucidity—miniscule sparks of clear-sightedness somewhere in between the bourgeois and the bohemian—capable of checking the reckless outpourings of certain victims of over-enthusiasm. It was a fortuitous measure because Patricio quickly began to tire of Paula.

His own reservations about her aside—and despite the way she dresses (overstated, provocative, even brassy)—, he has to admit that Paula plays an important role at the prestigious and elegant Verde

Mar Hotel. Not surprisingly, as long as she fulfills her public relations duties, the hotel management not only humors her and gives her whatever she wants, it actually encourages her amorous escapades with Patricio because "being the muse of a famous writer" cannot help but boost the prestige of the establishment.

All in all, Paula has no complications. Her future is ensured, her beauty is ensured and, she believes, the love of her life is ensured.

As for the hotel—which is increasingly frequented by Arab sheiks, American millionaires, and world famous actors—its clientele is also ensured, even in the winter months, thanks to its sports facilities, heated pools, and everything else the boundless imaginations of the jet set might desire. This is especially true since the brain behind the fortunate enterprise had the brilliant idea of distributing catalogs in the most scandalously rich locales worldwide, bearing the image of Paula, scantily clad and bursting with charm. It featured a catchphrase that caused an immediate furor, burying once and for all the worn-out "Spain Is Different." The slogan was, "Get to Know High-Voltage Spain." And Paula is right there to confirm the voltage promised by the Verde Mar Hotel.

"The inventor of this catalog should be congratulated. Now it is not so much that Spain is different, but that it 'surpasses' all of the other countries of the world equally," remarked Liaño once he got his hands on it.

"Surpasses and then some," Patricio responded.

However, the most perfect bodies and most finely tuned sexual fantasies can also lead to one's downfall. Maybe this is why, for a long time now Paula, despite her beauty, has been inadvertently expending Doctor Gallardo's ardor, which had once seemed so urgent and indestructible.

Now more than ever. Ever since he went down to the beach, Patricio has been vainly regarding her half naked body stretched out on the sand, and in vain she attempts to stir in him the combination of virulent tenderness and abusive devotion that used to fill her with happiness and faith in the future.

Now Paula is nothing more to him than a mannequin that moves and breathes as it methodically exposes itself to the rays of a sun liable to give it an inexorable case of skin cancer.

In reality, every potential source of pleasure is evaporating in the wake of Gregorio's unexpected telephone call from Thailand.

Nothing, not the transparency of the water or the delight Patricio takes in the warmth of the sand, or the aroma of mineral salts he has always associated with the most passionate moments of his life, can overcome his shock at hearing his son's voice again.

He seemed to fall into a stupor from the moment Leticia barged into his study without knocking and, voice quavering and eyes moist, motioned towards the telephone on his desk.

"Quickly, Doctor, grab the receiver. Your son is calling from Bangkok."

Doctor Gallardo did not react at first. He found it impossible to absorb what Leticia was saying.

"Come on, Doctor, please hurry. Gregorio wants to talk to you."

Occasionally Leticia has spells during which she is known to lose herself in the most outrageous fantasies. At that particular moment, however, she was speaking distinctly and firmly, and to prove she was telling the truth, she hastened to pick up the receiver and hand it to Patricio.

"Como on, Doctor. Don't just sit there."

Then he heard Gregorio's voice.

"Are you there, Dad?"

He responded, incredulous, "Is it really you, son? God, it's been so long since I've heard your voice."

Then he heard him clear his throat. There was no doubt about it. It was the classic sound that punctuated his son's speech whenever he was nervous.

"How are you, Dad?"

He asked it without much enthusiasm, as if out of courtesy rather than a genuine concern for his health.

"I'm fine. And you?"

Actually, Patricio's voice did not sound overly excited either. It is hard not to be guarded when we are not privy to the expressions of our interlocutor and with the chasm of three years of silence piquing our consciences.

"Fine, very well."

Then Gregorio went straight to the point.

"I'm calling to ask you for a favor. I need your help."

"Of course, son. How can I help you?"

Gregorio wasted no time on long, drawn out explanations.

"I've finally been given an important position at the Butantan Institute in São Paolo. Estrella and I are moving there immediately."

And after a few convincing explanations and roundabout, vaguely technical allusions, he went straight to the reason for his call.

"Could you take care of Miguel while Estrella and I get settled in

Brazil?"—and when his father did not respond right away—"You'd have the chance to get to know your grandson."

The truth is, when Patricio heard Miguel's name, he did not even recall he had a grandson.

"You're asking me to take care of your son?"

He was finding it hard to take it all in.

"Well, I can't imagine it would be a problem for you. He's intelligent. I don't think he'll give you any trouble. Leticia can take care of him."

He responded immediately.

"Of course I don't have a problem with it. To the contrary, I'd be delighted. When would you be sending him to me?"

Again, the feeling that he was dreaming and nothing he was hearing could be real.

"How long do you want him to stay with me?" he asked quickly.

"If it's not a problem, I'd like to leave him with you the whole summer. Estrella and I are going to need some time to take care of some pending matters and get accustomed to our new life."

Gregorio spoke rapidly, as if he were being prodded. He hoarded every second with his voice, leaving no room for Patricio to pose any as yet unanswered questions.

"I'm grateful you would entrust your son to me. You don't have to worry. I'll do everything I can to make sure he has a wonderful summer. But listen, son, I'd like to know why you've . . ."

But Gregorio was not about to let his father stray from the boundaries he was imposing.

"Don't ask questions, Dad."

Gregorio was right. It was dangerous to ask questions. It could jeopardize the magic of the moment—so out of context and yet so necessary—which Patricio had awaited for three years.

"I'm also grateful to you for your willingness to take charge of my son."—And before his father could respond—"I'd like to speak with Liaño. I need to give him instructions about the trip."

It seemed impossible that Gregorio could have mentioned Rodolfo with the naturalness of a good friend.

"Liaño is not at Mas Delfín right now, but when he returns I'll tell him to get in touch with you."

No, nothing is normal. Nothing has a plausible explanation. Maybe the passing of time, although it reinforces the pain, can also help us forget our follies. If not, how could Gregorio have so easily let go of the antagonism and hate he had felt towards Liaño six years

16

before? How could he have erased the provocations, attacks, and accusations that had turned Rodolfo into an undesirable presence during the course of that summer?

Yet none of those things seemed to be bothering his son now. It was as if that summer had never happened and his stay at Mas Delfín had been nothing more than a pleasant walk in the park.

"Now I would like to speak with Leticia."

He needed to fill her in on the child's habits, food preferences, interests and hobbies.

"And he should not forget to say his prayer before bed and when he wakes up in the morning."

"Don't worry, my boy. I'll take care of him just as I took care of you when you were little," responded Leticia.

He also suggested Miguel not be allowed to watch a lot of television.

"It dulls your brain."

"I'll do everything just as you say."

Then he asked to speak with his father again.

"The boy will be traveling alone. The flight attendants will look after him. All I ask is that Liaño go to the airport to pick him up."

There were a few disjointed, neutral and inconsequential comments, and then the goodbye.

"Goodbye, Dad. Thanks for helping me out."

Patricio tried to keep him on the phone, but to no avail. Gregorio was in a hurry. Gregorio was nothing more than a request: disembodied, faceless, unwilling to listen. Gregorio was just a voice. A voice somewhere in between commanding and callous, unwilling to dispel uncertainties or clarify realities. Its sole purpose was to impose and disconcert.

"You must be so happy, Doctor. Everything has finally worked itself out. If Gregorio is sending you the child, it must be because he is thinking about you and wants to make up for his silence."

Sometimes when Leticia is trying to be persuasive, it's as if she grabs onto a burning stick and ends up getting her hands burned.

"At least that's what I think."

But Patricio did not respond. He merely sat back down at his desk to contemplate the photograph of the grandson who would soon be by his side.

He also recalled the letter Gregorio had sent with the photograph of the boy. "He has his mother's dark eyes, but he's blond like you and me." And adding that Miguel had just turned two, "He seems older though. He's a sharp kid, aware of everything going on around him."

In those days, although Dula had died and Gregorio was remarried, communication between father and son remained fluid. Their conversation flowed effortlessly, the words stripped of pretense and perhaps even enriched by all that had transpired following the child's birth.

Patricio started. He refused to think about it. He told himself once again to think positively. The most important thing was to keep in mind that his son had called him on the telephone and had been civil, if remote, and had not hesitated to ask him for a favor.

Then he slowly prepared himself to go down to the beach where Paula was waiting.

It is not far to walk. The path meanders between thick rows of trees whose shade muffles the reverberations and serves as a buffer against weariness.

From the moment Patricio got there, Paula's reaction has not been at all what he anticipated. Sometimes Paula reacts hysterically without knowing why. She swings from submissive to acting the part of the fed up, peevish, tempestuous woman. She even starts to act out like some of those complex-laden, revenge-mongering feminists.

"So, soon I'm going to have to take care of this grandson of yours," she persists, without shifting her gaze from the sea.

"That will not be necessary. Leticia is prepared to care for him."

"What about you? What are you going to do?"

Patricio is on the verge of telling her that what he would really like to do is be alone on the beach. The Paula of this morning is irritating him beyond endurance. But he refrains. Sitting down beside her, he too allows his gaze to lose itself in the sea.

"I guess this Miguel is going to make life pretty complicated for us," she says.

"I don't see why."

"Come on. It's a pain to put up with a kid all summer."

"No one is asking you to put up with him."

Paula frowns. She does not like Patricio's response.

"You're not going to tell me you wouldn't mind it if I weren't around."

"You can do as you like. I'm not going to stop you, Paula."

She reacts instantaneously. She moves closer to him and strokes his head.

"Are you sure you won't need me?"

Patricio closes his eyes. The weight of her hand on his head is becoming intolerable.

"As far as I'm concerned, you can stay away until the boy leaves."

Suddenly, Paula is fawning.

"And you won't get bored without me?"

Patricio turns towards her with a sardonic look.

"I also get bored when I'm with you. Or hadn't you noticed?"

But Paula is not offended. She is convinced Patricio is joking.

"That's not a very nice answer."

"It wasn't meant to be. The fact is, most everyone gets bored, Paula. We are only entertained when life offers us something new. But the moment the new thing becomes routine, the boredom resurfaces."

Although Paula does not pick up on it right away, Patricio wants to hurt her. It is a form of revenge for her incessant insipidity and priggishness. He is impassive even as Paula looks at him now with the bemused expression of a woman unable to grasp how a man as passionate as Patricio can talk to her like that. Behave as if making love with her did not more than make up for all the ignorance for which he is constantly reproaching her.

"Don't get all worked up. In the end, 'to be bored' is not a pejorative verb. Without moments of boredom, no one would think. At least in my case, the more bored I get, the more I am apt to think. Ultimately, boredom is what gives birth to creativity."

Although Paula does not totally get it, what Patricio has said strikes her as convincing. And she is even grateful to him for speaking to her like that, because what he has said probably softens the harsh edge of his earlier insolence.

The truth is, when he is alone with Paula, Patricio nearly always has an irresistible urge to disorient and confuse her. He really couldn't say whether it was sadism or simply self defense against the affront of her insipid nature. Maybe it is because he is certain all he has to do is stretch out his hand and Paula will come running back for more.

"So you are often bored."

"Especially when I am not alone."

The look at each other. They smile. Often the most cutting insults are negated by a smile.

Even so, Paula changes the subject just in case.

"So Estrella and Gregorio are moving to Brazil."

"Apparently the snake farm in São Paolo is even more important than the one in Bangkok."

Paula shakes her head to indicate she will never understand the tastes of some scientists.

"He always has the blessed snake farm on his mind. I sometimes wonder what your son is looking for in that world of poisons. After all, poisons can't do anybody any good."

But Patricio is no longer listening to her.

The important thing is to examine the motive behind the telephone call, which he still has failed to grasp. And to think ahead about how to approach his grandson's arrival. And most of all, to find a way to make sure this connection with Gregorio never disintegrates again.

*　　*　　*

It has been a long night. Insomnia has taken hold of me just when I thought it would behoove me to close my eyes. And once insomnia has you in its grasp, there is no way to break free of it.

I've taken tranquilizers to no avail and vainly gone out onto the balcony of my study to contemplate the sea, which always acts as a sedative when I feel an excess of adrenaline rushing through me. The view tends to restore my calm and neutralize my anxieties.

But not tonight. Tonight, as I anticipated, the predatory memories have begun to stir. The scenes from the past are there, as sharp and as stabbing as if no time had elapsed at all, as if the lacerations of years past were stinging me once again.

My grandson Miguel. I never imagined Gregorio would ever ask me to take care of the boy. It's going to be just like having Gregorio back again when he was that age. Only Juliana was still alive then and caring for the child did not constitute as much of a responsibility.

At times like this Juliana becomes indispensable. If she had been around, none of what transpired probably would have happened and, naturally, Miguel would be better cared for when he arrived at Mas Delfín.

Gregorio feels the same way. I'm sure of it. In his mind, his mother was the perfect wife who took care of everything. How many times did he assure me he would never marry because he could not imagine finding a woman like her? Shortly after arriving in Bangkok, however, he announced that he had decided to get married. "You're not going to believe it, Dad, but I had to travel all the way to this blessed country to find the right woman."

For several months, Gregorio talked about little else when he called.

"She's changed my life, Dad. I never imagined that women like Dula existed." And he would begin to describe her with the attention to detail of a jeweler. "She's a doctor too, like us." Apparently she had graduated from the University of Chulalongkorn and was from an upstanding, Catholic, democratic family. Her father was Spanish, her mother Thai. "You'll come to the wedding, right, Dad?"

Everything between Gregorio and me was simple then and talking on the telephone had become such a deeply engrained habit that not to do so would have been strange indeed.

I soon received a photograph of the fiancée. She was not very tall and none of her features stood out particularly. I remember showing it to Rodolfo when I received it.

"What you have before you is my future daughter-in-law," I said.

"Liaño contemplated it for quite a while.

"She doesn't seem to be an ordinary woman," he said. "If it were possible to compare her to something other than a human, I would say she is like a closed door that conceals strange questions."

I did not understand what he was trying to say, but at the time, I was not concerned about what Rodolfo Liaño thought of Dula.

"Very appropriate for your son," he added. "She has an intelligent look about her."

When I regarded Dula's image, however, I saw nothing more than certain faintly oriental features, black hair, and enormous, slightly almond-shaped eyes

Gregorio never tired of singing her praises. "Dula's also interested in herpetological research, Dad." Apparently they had fallen in love while working together on a study involving some sort of reptile. But true love surfaced as they were collaborating on a venom extraction. "Strange, isn't it, Dad?"

The fact is, I was all set to travel to Thailand for the wedding when the accident happened.

Liaño described it as "one of those twists of fate" that sometimes intervene to ruin the best laid plans. The twist was actually an oncoming car that crashed head on into mine and came close to sending me directly into the next world.

The driver was an Englishman who had not quite figured out that driving on the right side of the road was slightly more involved than simply doing the opposite of what was done in his country.

Outcome: one broken leg, a dislocated arm, and the usual bumps and bruises, all of which absolutely precluded my trip to Thailand.

I remember that Gregorio—obsessed about not getting married if I were not present—tried to change the wedding date. I wouldn't hear of it. "I'm not going let you change your plans all because of that son of a . . . Brit." Even Dula was willing to wait until I had recovered. "I would have liked to have met you in person before the wedding," she told me on the telephone.

In the end, however, they got married without me.

Afterward, there were even more telephone calls. "Are you feeling better, Dad?" And he quickly turned to talking about the woman he had married. "I don't know whether she's pretty or not, Dad. I just know there is no other woman like her." He often said Dula was made of a substance unlike other members of her sex. "I'm telling you, she's different, Dad. When you meet her, you'll see what I mean." The truth is, when Gregorio started in about Dula he became so talkative it was hard to get him off the phone. "Come on, son, hang up already. This is going to cost you a fortune."

Four years went by. Four years of constant exchanges of ideas, opinions, consultations. Gregorio seemed happy. It was obvious in the way he laughed, tossed jokes in my direction, or shared his never-ending doubts with me. "Do you think Dula would like it if I gave her an emerald broach shaped like a snake?" or "Maybe for Christmas I'll put together a collection of all your books bound in leather. Dula thinks books should have a dignified appearance, especially if they are important, like yours. But, what color do you think I should choose?"

Clearly his characteristic self-doubt was as deeply ingrained as ever. "Come on, son. Decide once and for all to stand on your own two feet. Don't discount your own opinions. You're too smart to doubt every step you take."

I remember on one occasion I took the risk of inquiring when they thought they might make me a grandfather. But I understood immediately that I should never have asked. Gregorio's tone became somber and his response struck me as somewhat clipped. "Whenever God wills it. We want it as much as you do."

But the desire never crystallized and as the years slipped by, the marriage produced nothing more than scientific discoveries.

The telephone calls continued, however, and our camaraderie only became stronger. Sometimes Gregorio even allowed himself to make jokes that crossed the boundaries of a father-son relationship. But the fact was, the ties between us were those of a steadfast and solid friendship more than anything else. "I'm worried that you haven't remarried, Dad. What's wrong with all the women? Have they all turned into Lesbians?"

I had not yet met Paula at the time. "It's not their fault. I still have some close women friends. But you already know what my problem is. None of them could ever replace your mother."

So many things had transpired in the four years preceding that summer.

Without my really being aware of it, my books had begun to collect awards. They were translated into other languages and became the subject of numerous literary studies, all of which Rodolfo assiduously collected, "so your future grandchildren will know who their grandfather was." He did not seem to realize that the future was here and my grandchildren were conspicuous by their absence. But there was still room for hope at the time and Rodolfo never wavered in his optimism.

I can see him now, coming into my study with the self-assured air that Gregorio used to find so exasperating as he approaches my desk and regards Dula's photograph. "It's hard to imagine such a fragile, diminutive woman could be such an important doctor," he joked.

Rodolfo Liaño has always been one to tell the truth even when it stings. "One shouldn't beat around the bush. The truth is like iodine: it's only painful when it is curing you." Yet the truth about Dula never managed to cure him. To the contrary. He ended up converting that truth into one of the most painful lies of his life. That's why whenever he mentions her he tries so hard to convert my daughter-in-law into something akin to a fantasy. "She was meant to be air but someone screwed up and changed her into fire."

I must admit that I'm sometimes puzzled by Rodolfo. Although he has always been like an open book to me—after years of observing his gestures, his whims, his tics and even the inflections of his voice—there are blank pages in the book of his life and I have never been able to discover what confessions Rodolfo would have written on them.

In the old days it was different. Before, it would have been enough to observe his expression—incapable of masking his emotions—or the way he bit his upper lip, or simply watch him try to smile when he was down, to discover the true state of his feelings, some fleeting concession to weakness, or his hidden heroism.

Only afterward did Rodolfo become opaque to me. Particularly when Gregorio, blinded with rage, heaped such misery upon him, all of which he bore stoically and without complaint.

Be that as it may, there is no way I could do without Rodolfo. A good secretary, he knows how to organize and anticipate and, most importantly, he is a true public relations wizard.

His abilities are boundless. He plays bridge, tennis, golf, and padel. He can fill in for me in any venue I absolutely cannot endure, and he has no equal when it comes to women. His presence, his impeccable education, and the good taste inculcated in him since childhood lend him a particular aura that drives women wild.

He never argues. "For what? Arguing is just a by-product of pride," he likes to say. "Argument—and our ability to take offense—destroy the effectiveness of the experience." And with a resigned expression, "Truthfully, Patricio, nothing would wound me more than to forfeit my right to experience. It is so hard to acquire it in the first place."

I still get emotional when I recall the day Gregorio announced that he and Dula were finally going to spend their vacation at Mas Delfín. It was to be an extended vacation—from early July to the end of September—as they had not had a decent break since their wedding. "We'll have to plan an unforgettable summer for the kids. Five years is a long time to be away," remarked Rodolfo.

And with his accustomed efficiency, he began to oversee the needed repairs at Mas Delfín so Gregorio and his wife could take full advantage of everything the farmstead had to offer.

The household was suddenly in a turmoil. Even Leticia took it upon herself to make sure "master Gregorio does not miss the attentions the missus always lavished upon him, may she rest in peace." Leticia has always liked to evoke Juliana's name as often as possible. She has the notion that a sort of resurrection takes place every time she says it. At least this is Rodolfo's explanation. "Memory is what resuscitates our deceased loved ones."

I remember that July as part of a scorching, schizophrenic summer with constant wildfires.

And there was another distressing incident as well: the disappearance of Brutus, the mastiff Juliana had raised from a puppy and who had always accompanied me on my rounds at the farm. He vanished suddenly, as if the ground had swallowed him up. No one had any idea where he could have gone off to. We were totally baffled. We began to think he may have tumbled from the bluffs but Canuto, the groundskeeper, who was an expert climber, searched the most inaccessible crevices and found no trace of the animal.

Other than that, there was every indication that a perfect summer was in the making. The cherry trees were bursting with swollen, dark, juicy fruit. And then there was the solemn majesty of the woods, richly adorned with flowers and leaves.

Notwithstanding the heat and the wildfires, there had been plenty of rain that year and—although the eternally discontented might grouse about how nature had been bloated by so much rain and yes, of course droughts were bad, but too much rain was worse because the vegetation grew out of control and when all the leaves dried they caused wildfires—the truth is, the countryside had never been so beautiful as it was that summer nor the air so pure.

Then there was the greenhouse. The strange temple of flowers and plants that Juliana had bequeathed us was once again brimming with vitality, just as it had been when its mistress was alive and visiting there was like entering a luminous tunnel latticed with various perfumes, which penetrated the lungs as if to dilate them with a newfound restlessness.

I still recall exactly how I felt that morning when I woke up and realized Gregorio was finally coming to Spain after five long years of absence.

What I felt wasn't just happiness, plain and simple. It was so much more. Perhaps a sort of pride coated with the tenderness I had always felt towards my son, and all of it wrapped up in my eagerness to see him again, to look in his eyes, and to hear his voice free of interference from those contraptions invented by men to cheat time and space.

I remember when I rose, I stood before the mirror for quite a while, wondering what Gregorio would think of my appearance. I wasn't bad looking. The gray hairs were mostly hidden among the blond and my blue eyes shown clear against my tanned skin.

I went down to the terrace to survey the road that zigzagged downhill towards the esplanade alongside the house. The air was clear and the still, sun-soaked atmosphere lent an aura of serenity to the countryside, the sea, and the woods.

Everything was quiet. Even the sounds of the sea seemed to come from afar, so much so that the rustle of the treetops, the trills of the birds and the remote screeching of the seagulls drowned out the pounding of the waves.

Suddenly the grind of a motor descending the hill absorbed all other sound.

I quickly jumped over the hedge to meet the car.

I think Leticia, Rosario and Canuto were running across the esplanade behind me.

*   *   *

When Gregorio descended from the car, the two of us just stood there face to face, paralyzed, as if some unseen catch was keeping us from moving. Nothing seemed real. It was as if we were dreaming.

Then the embrace. And the wordless emotion, our throats constricted by a grief drowning in joy that rendered us incapable of speech.

Later the exclamations, disjointed, fragmented by the shock of seeing each other again. And the slaps on the back. And a whole world of things tumbling all over each other to get out, translated into meaningless exclamations, which gradually and by dint of common sense, reclaimed their right to be actual words.

Then came Leticia's hugs, her tears, her expressions of emotion, the caresses of a sentimental old lady.

"At last, my boy, at last."

And Canuto's greetings, both subservient and bold, because he too had known my son since he was a little boy, "Look at you, lad. All grown up."

Rosario was there too, smiling as she unloaded the suitcases. "She's the new maid," explained Leticia.

No one remembered Dula. No matter how hard I try, I cannot place her at that moment. She had probably remained by the car door chatting with Rodolfo Liaño, because Rodolfo had in fact picked them up at El Prat airport.

I cannot even reconstruct our meeting when Gregorio said, "Dad, this is Dula." I can only recall my son's voice telling me about her, but I have no memory of the details or what I might have said to her or she to me. I have no idea whether I kissed her or held out my hand. It is as if something more powerful than my memory had sought to erase every trace of the scene.

The only thing I have not forgotten is her perfume: the unmistakable scent of violets which suddenly overtook all of the other fragrances of the countryside.

The truth is, Dula was nothing more than a form to me at the time—albeit a pleasant one—lacking in color, sound, or dimension. Naturally, the only thing on my mind was having my son back with me again, completely grown into a man. And to hear his voice, admire his mature aspect. No, right then I was not thinking about anything else. To have done so would not have fit who I was. To

26

have done so might have indicated an unbalanced mind with sick and twisted inclinations.

And I have to say in all honesty that the last thing on my mind would have been to turn down such dubious alleyways. To step into traps that would expose me to losing myself in ways that were an anathema to someone wholeheartedly committed to Gregorio's happiness.

Still, I cannot understand how I could have completely blanked out the details of that particular meeting. The inability to recall certain details can be as inexplicable as the vapors rising from the ground after a summer rain that, despite their density, evaporate in an instant.

As a matter of fact, I had no real interaction with my daughter-in-law until dinner time, when Dula, after having spent a good deal of time in the bedroom unpacking, came down to the sitting room where her husband, Liaño, and I had been talking since their arrival.

All at once I saw her there, dressed in a diaphanous white outfit and treading softly perhaps not wanting to interrupt our exchange. It occurred to me then that Dula did not seem like a flesh and blood woman, but resembled instead some vaporous substance in the shape of a woman.

I am seeing her now, her discreet gesture indicating we should not get up so as not to disturb the conversation. And then I see her curling up against her husband's leg as she settles herself on the floor.

Clearly she did not wish to draw attention to herself. And, although the subjects under discussion were not directly related to her, she was obviously interested. It was obvious in the way she gazed at her husband, in the pleasure she took in his happiness as he conjured up memories of his childhood and adolescence.

"Do you remember the laboratory I set up in the attic?"

It was all a thing of the present once more.

"It drove your mother crazy," I told him. "She couldn't stand all the lizards and bugs inside those little boxes on the table."

Gregorio laughed. God, how often I'd yearned to hear his laugh again.

"You know why, Dad? Because of their venom. I've always been fascinated by poisonous animals. Maybe some day we'll know exactly why God made certain animals that way. It's intrigued me ever since I was a little kid. That's why I was so attracted to scorpions, tarantulas, spiders, and snakes."

Dula smiled as he talked. Her smile was like the letter v, magnetic, hinting at a world of secrets her finely formed, unpainted lips refused to confess.

Then dinner arrived, served by Leticia: scorpene a la marinara, chicken croquettes and strawberry ice cream.

"All of your favorite dishes, my boy," she said as we took our places at the table.

Gregorio was clearly pleased.

"The truth is I couldn't even remember what Spanish food tasted like. You've outdone yourself, Leticia."

It was a dinner replete with long-forgotten events, which became real and joyful in the atmosphere of the evening. It was as if everything we recalled had never been lost at all during the preceding four years.

After dinner, we went out onto the terrace. The sea sounded subdued and somewhat plaintive in the distance. Dula excused herself early, saying she was tired and knew Gregorio would want some time alone with his father after such a long separation.

Rodolfo apparently took this as a hint. "You're wife is quite right. I'm going to leave you as well." And as Dula headed for the door, Rodolfo followed.

That was the first time I noticed something like a cloud in my son's gaze. Certain meaningless details sometimes acquire extremely important dimensions for no apparent reason. But the cloud quickly dissipated and Gregorio and I returned to our chat with no other thought than to recapture old times and convert them into present realities. "Remember when we bought you the bicycle? And the water skis, and those rafts?

It was a long night, but our happiness made it feel much too short. There was so much to tell. So much to probe. And so much to discover.

The waters were still calm then and there was nothing to indicate that life was going to take the twist it took or such clear-cut futures could become stunted overnight. It was also beyond imagining that Dula's youth would be cut short within a year in the process of giving birth to the son for whom she had so desperately longed.

At the time, all of this was utterly remote, utterly nothing. No one had any reason to believe that time would seize upon us and trample us the way it has, or that the future lying in wait for us would conspire to separate me from my son in such a drastic manner. The truth is, nothing special happened that evening that would have given us any inkling of the trap fate was setting for us.

Or perhaps it was not a trap. More likely, it was the logical outcome when we allow ourselves to plunge into the abyss, certain we will suddenly sprout wings and emerge unscathed from our moment of carelessness. A simple closing of the eyes so as not to see the danger. A covering of the ears so as not to hear the warnings that reason is screaming at us.

And maybe also a consequence of our selfishness. How should I know? It can be so many things.

2

Paula has remained at the hotel this morning. Patricio has made it clear to her that he would prefer to await his grandson's arrival alone. "Forget the swim, Paula. I'm not planning to go down to the beach. Anyway, your presence might confuse him." And following the established pattern, Paula had acquiesced without protest.

Now, settled in one of the lounge chairs on the terrace in the shade of a cork oak tree, Patricio Gallardo reflects on how slowly time seems to pass sometimes.

The hours must be dragging and weighing on Miguel too. He'll probably be exhausted when he arrives. He will have spent over fifteen hours in the air flying Thai-International airlines from Bangkok to Madrid, including a one-hour layover in Rome and a change of planes before landing in Barcelona around mid-morning. And this does not even count the five hour time difference, or the ride from Bangkok to Donmuang airport and from El Prat Airport to the Costa Brava. A rough trip for such a little boy, thinks his grandfather.

Leticia is also of the opinion that Miguel should not have been making the trip on his own.

"His father should have traveled with him."

Sometimes Leticia rubs salt into the wound without realizing how much it might hurt.

"The flight attendants will watch out for him."

"But the child doesn't know them. He's going to be lonely."

Patricio thinks Leticia is right, but refuses to get into a discussion with her over a matter that is also a sore point with him.

The truth is, ever since his son announced the arrival of his grandson, Patricio has done nothing else but imagine what the boy must be like, since all he has is a photograph taken when he was two.

Three years have elapsed and children tend to change dramatically at that age.

Surely his looks and gestures—while in part inherited reflexes—must also owe something to his surroundings, to the thousand external battles copied from grown-ups to defend against those other internal battles that often besiege children.

It is also possible that his features or traits are merely "contagions" from somebody close to him, or birthmarks inherited from some distant relation who never dreamed of having a descendent called Miguel who was the grandson of a Spanish writer.

"It won't be long now, Doctor. Mr. Liaño called from Barcelona over a half hour ago to say the plane had just landed."

Of course Patricio wonders what percentage Miguel has inherited from his father and his mother and what proportion of the genes from one or the other will propel the child towards his future.

"I suppose the poor creature will be starving."

Leticia is always on top of the food issue. She has taken matters well in hand and, just in case, has prepared all kinds of food to satisfy any possible appetite the little one might have.

"You have to please the stomach, Doctor."

"I don't think it will be necessary. Surely the flight attendants will have taken care of it."

But Leticia is reluctant to trust in the flight attendants' abilities. What is more, she has her doubts about airline food.

"I don't set much store by those young girls who are in charge of the children. What can they possibly know about the needs of a little boy? Just look at them. They're all just like sticks themselves. I'll bet they don't even eat right."

Be that as it may, Patricio thinks there are several obscure areas he fails to understand when it comes to his grandson. Why have Gregorio and his new wife allowed Miguel to travel by himself? Why couldn't they have taken a few days off from their move to Brazil to make a detour to Spain, even if just to keep the little one from feeling so abandoned?

He also fails to grasp how a five year old child can constitute a bother for a young couple—with enough income to hire a nanny—no matter how complicated the move from Bangkok to São Paolo.

"Surely Gregorio wanted to take advantage of the occasion to give you a chance to get to know your grandson," Leticia tries to explain.

"It's possible."

In the end, he thinks now, no matter how much Gregorio might have cut himself off, the bond that had always united them wasn't going to break over night. Maybe Gregorio was trying, through his son, to keep the bond between him and his father from being permanently severed.

It's better not to think, he tells himself. It's better to let that summer go and turn fully towards the future. Ultimately, Miguel is the future too. A future free of sorrows.

The rest—the thing that has been piquing his conscience ever since Gregorio reconnected with him—must be regarded as the spoils of the dead. It doesn't matter that the woods he is contemplating from the terrace look exactly the same as the woods of years past, although the trees have grown, or that the esplanade adjacent to the house was the scene of Dula and Gregorio's arrival six years before, or that Daní mountain still conceals the hermitage of a saint with no name. ("Why don't you make up a name for the saint, Dula?") Immaterial that their boundless conversations night after July night on the terrace where he now sits, facing the same sea he now faces, have been swept away by the north winds, or the southwest winds, or simply by the weight of the years. The important thing now is to make an effort and try to forget.

"Too bad Brutus isn't with us any more," Leticia persists. "Miguel would have enjoyed playing with him."

But Brutus was gone too, along with his affection and cleverness, his enthusiastic panting, and his slobbery licks.

"If Miguel likes dogs, I can buy him one."

The bad thing about Leticia is her proclivity to interfere where she is not wanted. That is why Doctor Gallardo sometimes gets fed up and begs her to leave him in peace.

"The poor boy is going to feel so uprooted. We have to do everything possible to make sure he doesn't suffer."

"Of course, Leticia. We will do whatever is necessary."

Moreover, while always well-intentioned, Leticia is incapable of figuring out when she is intruding and when she is needed. She has always felt she has the right to offer her opinion at any time and in any circumstance affecting the family. What is more, she frequently mistakes her own need to vent for the conviction that she is indispensable.

"And during the town festival, we'll have to take him to see all the attractions."

"Naturally."

Patricio closes his eyes. As everyone in the household is aware, when Doctor Gallardo is tired of chitchat he closes his eyes as if he is going to take a nap. But Leticia still has not noticed this subtle manner of disengaging. She continues to speak, even though the doctor has just about had his fill.

"I suppose you won't be writing as long as the little one is here at Mas Delfín."

"You suppose correctly, Leticia. I had already thought of it."

33

"Then it would be good if you could spend a little more of your time getting Canuto to shape up."

And she gestures towards the greenhouse, which still stands there by the bluff. although it has fallen into a state of almost total disrepair.

"Just look it Doctor. It's practically a ruin."

"Things age, Leticia. You can't blame it all on Canuto."

For a long while now, Patricio has been noticing that the place is turning into a skeleton. The wear and tear from the wind and the rains, the humidity from the mineral salts, the dust clinging to the glass panes, and the rusted metal, have all conspired to turn the once resplendent place into a sort of shipwreck, unable to remain afloat.

Patricio no longer really cares whether the plants are healthy and vital. Maybe because they just bloom and die without anyone to notice their decline or lavish such rare affection upon them as Juliana once had.

Even now, as Patricio contemplates the pavilion, something deep inside is urging him to make it disappear.

It has lived too long, he tells himself. And anything that lives too long ends up inspiring contempt or indifference.

Which is why now, when Paula decides to cut any flowers that happen to still bloom by the hand of God, Patricio does not get angry as before. He even lets her fill the house with vases full of sprays because, according to her, a house without flowers is like a coop without chickens. "It has no reason to exist."

In contrast, Juliana never allowed a single flower to be yanked from its stem. She asserted in no uncertain terms that from the moment they sprout, plants—just as any other living thing—needed their own place to live. "It isn't right to decorate the rooms with life forms, Patricio. And plants are living beings."

Patricio no longer even minds when Paula, carried away by her romantic whims and "feminine" foibles, tries to mimic the pedestrian habits of people who, convinced of their impeccably refined taste, blunder willy-nilly into the most tactless realms.

"Canuto does what he can, Leticia. He even plays the record player to keep the flowers from wilting prematurely."

"I don't understand you, doctor. After the missus died, you said we had to do everything possible to keep the greenhouse from getting old."

"But everything gets old, Leticia. Nothing is eternal."

And he abruptly recalls something Dula—still sheathed in an invisible armor that shielded the beating of her heart and lent her a deathlike aspect—told him for no reason. "The word 'always' is the most effective disguise for the word 'never'." It's as if he can see her, getting into the boat where Rodolfo and Gregorio are already chatting amiably, as he extends his hand to her from the stern to help her aboard. "Come on Dula, grab onto me."

Everything still seemed harmless then, the evening conversations filled with seemingly innocuous allusions interspersed with companionable silences.

It was the beginning of July and Mas Delfín was still the bucolic Garden of Eden, with no forbidden trees—as Rodolfo would say—and no snakes other than those Gregorio and Dula described as they recounted their experiences at the Bangkok snake farm.

"The snakes sometimes fight among themselves, but when they do, neither of the two survives," his son liked to explain. "One of them always swallows the other and is asphyxiated in the process." It was a Dantean nightmare. To die from swallowing. To feel yourself swallowed as you die. It was two monsters facing off, neither one of them with a chance of emerging victorious.

He remembers listening as they described it. The four of them were on the terrace—Paula was a superficial love interest at the time, someone whose charms had inflamed the writer, but to whom he had not yet flung opened the doors of Mas Delfín—and the night was incandescent. It was one of those clear nights that turn the sea into a huge reservoir of dark ink.

Suddenly, Dula's voice, "Well, let's not go overboard. Snakes haven't always been considered malevolent and ill-fated." She immediately launched into an account of the positive features of the ophidians. "Remember how God directed Moses to sculpt a bronze snake so the Israelites who gazed upon it after suffering a snakebite would become immune to the venom?"

At the time, Dula was still the serene, happy woman who concocted unexpected and charming explanations as she sat curled up against her husband's legs, allowing him to stroke her hair with the naturalness of a gesture that has become habit.

"In ancient civilizations, snakes were considered munificent beings. They were believed to be very wise, and imbued with certain kinds of knowledge, magical powers, and even therapeutic properties."

When Dula spoke—always in her silky voice that sounded as if it had just been rescued from silence—the others remained quiet.

It wasn't just out of interest in what she was saying, but how she said it.

No one else expressed themselves the way she did. And despite the fragility of her voice, no one commanded the same attention when they spoke. It was interesting to observe the disconnect between her appearance—petite, with a penetrating, smiling expression, gentle features, eyes slightly tilted yet large and vivacious—and her words: sure, firm, grounded.

Her opinions were remarkably devoid of even the slightest hint of arrogance. She offered them good-naturedly, as if she were more interested in the response than the point she was making. Then there were her gestures, always slow and harmonious, her cheerful expressions, and the special way she had of resting her head on her husband's knee as she massaged his ankle and calf.

"Have you noticed what Dula's like, Dad?" he would ask his father. "Always ready to surprise us with something new."

Dula was tactful too. If she sensed her husband and father-in-law needed to discuss a particular subject after having spent so many years apart, she would find a way to excuse herself. To no avail did husband and father-in-law invite her to stay. "The eleventh is 'thou shalt not disturb,'" she would say smilingly and then vanish as softly as she had come.

She even made an effort not to intrude when they went down to the beach for a swim, especially after Paula began to visit Mas Delfín at the accustomed beach time.

The first time it happened, the ever-discreet Dula reacted like a woman on the verge of indiscretion.

"I guess Paula is your girlfriend, right?"

Which was exactly what Paula was becoming. Patricio had been seeing her for about two weeks and her presence at Mas Delfín proved was proof that their relationship was something more than a mere friendship.

"We are dating," Patricio responded.

Dula nodded and tried to be pleasant.

"She is very pretty," she said. "I can see why you're attracted to her."

And without waiting for a response, she implored Liaño to help her climb the hillocks ringing the beach so she could take in the view from atop the bluff.

Rodolfo was always willing to please her. "It's like helping a dragonfly," he joked. "Sometimes I have the impression that Dula is weightless."

In contrast, not only was Paula not weightless, she was working hard to be considered a woman "of substance," someone who deserved attention because the perfection of her body demanded it. "Come on Patricio, I dare you to take a swim with me." She did not realize that what Patricio really liked to do was to sit on the beach, gaze into the distance, and immerse himself in the themes he was going to develop in his next book. "Okay Paula." And he forced himself to join her in the water so Paula—the recently discovered, incredibly beautiful Paula—would not grow tired of him.

What was really interesting, however, was to observe Paula and Dula side by side. Suddenly, neither the beauty of the former nor the unassuming appearance of the latter was what one noticed at first glance. They actually seemed to exchange roles. It was as if their bodies and faces blurred and their features detached themselves and took off in search of a different being and a more authentic reason to exist.

Sometimes when father and son were alone, their habit of sharing confidences naturally led them to discuss the two women. "Paula is like a trophy, right Dad?" Gregorio had hit on it. Paula could be nothing else to him. He had begun to realize it now that his macho vanity had been satisfied and Paula was gradually becoming less of an agreeable presence and more a difficult burden to bear.

Strive as she might to become the irreplaceable companion which fate had bestowed upon the writer, Paula was nothing more than a monolith or a sphinx. A dolmen installed in his life to adorn it with something ancient and marvelous, but incapable of reason.

"On the other hand, Dula is the hidden beauty," he remembered telling Gregorio. "It's as if nature wanted to endow her with riches beyond the suppleness of her body and mind." And seeing his son was pleased, "I can't think of any other way to explain it, Gregorio."

Yes, Gregorio still smiled during those days and he took in everything Patricio said with the same contentment with which he had always received his father's opinions. "I knew you would like Dula when you met her, Dad."

On one occasion, as Dula headed into the waves, Gregorio could not stop staring at her. One had the impression he was absorbing rather than watching her, so that her image would remain engraved on his retina forever. "You really love her, don't you, Son?" And without taking his eyes off the diminutive figure, he assented as if he were talking to himself instead of his father, "I couldn't live without her."

The same day, Gregorio had also confided to him that what had most attracted him to Dula was how much she resembled Juliana. "Mom was also sweet, devoted, serene, and full of good sense. And she was religious like Dula. Maybe that's why I fell in love with her."

Patricio Gallardo, however, was not so sure there was a resemblance between Dula and Juliana. There was a wider gap between his own wife's intelligence and her goodness than that bridging Dula's intelligence and her gentleness.

His daughter-in-law's intellect was too quick, too sharp to be fooled by appearances and sentiments as Juliana's had been. Despite her gentleness, the wisdom displayed by Gregorio's wife probably predominated over her other qualities.

Patricio was therefore convinced that if his son had been unfaithful to Dula—as he himself had been during Juliana's lifetime—it was unlikely Dula would have forgiven Gregorio as easily as his own wife had forgiven him.

Doctor Gallardo yawns suddenly. Leticia's monotone, replete with invectives against Canuto for his failure to keep up the greenhouse as Juliana had intended, is adding to the lethargy he has been feeling ever since he settled into the lounge chair there on the terrace.

"The dear departed missus always said that improving on nature is a way of cooperating with God. But for some time now, Canuto has not been cooperating. Because of him, the natural life in the pavilion is becoming a natural death."

But Doctor Gallardo is no longer listening.

Doctor Gallardo has just drifted into the deepest sleep. He is aware of nothing more than a hodgepodge of memories, expectations, consciences, and uprootings blending into the sound of the waves. Actually, Doctor Gallardo is dreaming. It is a strange, absurd dream and it seems real, even though it is just the transitory state of a memory deformed.

So when Rodolfo Liaño arrives back at Mas Delfín with his grandson in the car, not even the hubbub raised by Leticia, Canuto, and Rosario wakes him. He is awakened, in fact, by a light, nervous weight on his chest and the brush of moist lips on his cheek.

He unexpectedly breathes in a peculiar scent. It is the normal scent of a somewhat sweaty boy, which calls to mind Gregorio when he was little.

And then Leticia's voice.

"Come on, Miguel, give your grandfather another kiss and let's see if he opens his eyes."

The kisses are timid and fleeting, a little forced. But what Patricio notices when he opens his eyes is the dark gaze that seems to bore into his.

"Miguel?"

And Leticia, always a nuisance, "Well who else would it be, Doctor?"

Doctor Gallardo sits up to contemplate his grandson. He can see right away that the child is bewildered. Even though the woman called Leticia has told him at least a thousand times that the man sleeping in the lounge chair is his grandfather, he can't seem to figure out what the devil the word means.

During the trip from Barcelona to Mas Delfín, Rodolfo Liaño had tried to clarify the concepts for him. "Your grandfather is your father's father." But, although he asks no questions, Miguel fails to grasp how it is possible that an old man, such as the one half asleep before him, can be somebody's "dad."

"Come closer, Miguel. I want to get a better look at you."

But the child does not move. He too is fascinated by this blond, blue-eyed man with the deeply grooved face who reminds him so much of his father.

"You're tired, right, Miguel?"

Tired is another word that does not seem right. To his way of thinking, you can only get tired when you run a lot, or play soccer, or in nursery school when they make the kids do gym. But how could he be tired when he's been sleeping almost the whole way since he left Bangkok?

"No, I'm not tired."

He says it firmly, irritably. The word "tired" is offensive to him. Sometimes grown-ups can make kids really angry just because they don't get how much it hurts to be wrongly accused of something.

"I don't get tired," he insists.

And then the laughter. Another example of disrespect that Miguel cannot stand for. To laugh at what he says is even more insulting than asking him whether he is tired. What especially pains him is Leticia's laughter. The tubby woman with the puffed up face has been plaguing him with kisses ever since he arrived and calling him "my boy." Why the devil would that woman think he was any boy of hers? Miguel knows that he is only the child of his parents. He has always known it. So there is no reason for a fat old lady like Leticia to start calling him that.

"You must be hungry, right, Miguel?"

Miguel hesitates. He is not sure how he should respond to that one. You never can tell with grown-ups. He finally makes a decision.

"I don't know."

And the laughter grows. He is now surrounded by an eruption of chuckles, teasing comments, and noisy banter that sounds to him like jeering.

"So you don't know."

But when Leticia attempts to approach him, the child backs away abruptly, as if fearing that a woman so disinclined to be nice might hurt him.

"I don't like you," he yells at her. "I don't like you at all. And if you laugh at me I'm going to laugh at you too."

And suddenly, for no other reason than the indignation which has gradually been welling up in him, he bursts out crying. It is a violent, sudden, exaggerated wail. More than crying, one might say it was an explosion of trapped anger or suppressed fear.

The grandfather reacts at once. Taking the boy into his arms, he clutches him to his chest and covers his face with kisses.

"Please don't cry, Miguel. We all love you. No one is laughing at you."

But the child does not listen. He has reached the limits of his endurance and he has no desire to keep on pretending he is a big, smart boy, as he has been ever since he left Thailand.

He's been putting up with seeing unfamiliar faces and hearing unfamiliar voices too long to remain calm as he promised his father he would when they said goodbye. "Remember, Miguel, you have to behave like a big boy, all grown up." The devil take big boys, and grown-ups, and all the well-known tricks they use to fool little kids like him.

As far as he can tell, none of the people around him is worth the trouble of pretending something he doesn't feel. And right then, the last thing Miguel feels is calm and composed.

Besides, he's fed up with so many changes, transfers, boarding and deboarding, uniformed young women smiling at him and offering him candy. Too many sudden changes of environment, of airports. Too much traipsing down endless hallways and hearing loudspeakers announcing the names of strange places, and contemplating long lines of faceless people waiting for who knew what. Fed up, too, with observing people in a hurry yelling at lost people, or announcing flight numbers or pronouncing undecipherable names.

"Please Miguel. Stop crying. Don't be upset. No one wants to hurt you. Look at me little fellow. I'm your dad's dad and I'll always defend you against anything bad." And as he speaks, he motions for the others to leave them alone. "Do you hear me, Miguel? Come on, lean against me."

And as the child sobs, he rocks him in his arms like a baby. Later, as the boy begins to calm down, he sits him in the lounge chair and lays his arm across his back.

"Take a good look at me. I'm not a stranger. I want you to be sure of that."

Miguel, his cheeks damp, his eyes glistening, and his face flushed, regards him with slightly less distrust.

"My God, you look just like your mother."

Dula is there in the boy's features, his expressions, in everything about him.

It is a different Dula—a blond one, the eyes not as tilted—yet still Dula, who sometimes regarded him with the same half-timorous, half-trusting look.

"Mom?"

The child does not understand what his grandfather has said. No one has ever told him he looks like his mother.

"You know my mom?"

Once again the bewilderment and the fear of stepping into more traps designed to expose him to further ridicule.

"When did you see my mom?" he asks, curious. He may be inexperienced, but Miguel is no dummy and he knows that this man who claims to be his grandfather cannot possibly know his mother. "You've never been to Bangkok. My dad told me so."

"But she was here at Mas Delfín."

"When?"

"Before you were born."

"No she wasn't."

Miguel is quite sure of this too. His mother has told him more than once that she had never visited Spain.

Doctor Gallardo suddenly realizes that he and Miguel are not referring to the same person.

"To a certain extent, you are correct. The mother you have now has never come to Spain. I am referring to your real mother. Your father assured me that you know Estrella is not your real mother."

41

His grandfather's response leaves the boy pensive. He could be right. But there is so much evidence to indicate that Estrella is indeed a real mother. One look at his canvas boots is enough to persuade him.

The child suddenly lifts his legs and shows his grandfather the boots.

"My mom gave them to me."

It's his way of affirming that only an authentic mother can give gifts as important as a pair of canvas boots.

"Her name is Estrella, right? And when the child nods—"you're right. I don't know that mom," confirms Patricio. "I was referring to your mom from before."

"The one that lives up there?" And he points towards the sky.

"That's right. The one who lives up there."

But he can tell from the way Miguel says it that the woman up there is not a mother. Is not anything at all for that matter.

"Her name was Dula."

The boy shrugs. The name is neither strange nor familiar. It is just a name. A hollow word which occasionally comes up when the grown-ups talk about the past, but really is just an excuse for the photograph his father placed on his bedside table with little explanation.

"There is no way you could remember her," his grandfather continues. "She died when you were born."

"So she couldn't be my mom."

In the boy's opinion, no one can be considered a person if they don't have a body and don't live anywhere. And to him Dula is just that: a photograph with no voice, no opinions, and no feelings. On the other hand, Estrella exists. She has volume. She takes him to school, buys him clothes, gives him presents and rewards him with ice cream or stickers when he is good.

"My mom talks, you know? She isn't dead like the other one."

He has to justify his arguments somehow and to Miguel's way of thinking, the fact that Dula has died disqualifies her from motherhood.

"Besides, I don't want the mom I have now to die," observes the child. "And if I don't want her to, she won't."

Of course what Miguel needs is a mother who is alive, who envelops him in her embrace, kisses him, and repeats over and over again how much she loves him. He cannot accept that any of his loved ones might be mute, consigned to being silent effigies like the dark and empty photograph his father placed on the bed table.

"My mom loves me."

His tone is firm. He is not about to let his grandfather believe he isn't worthy of being loved by a mother. It is a matter of honor or dignity to him, although he cannot really explain why.

"We all love you, Miguel."

But the boy does not seem to be in agreement. To him the word "love" goes hand in hand with "live." He is certain that the dead, by virtue of being so, are unable to feel love because the distance keeps them from coming close to the living and taking care of them the way Estrella takes cares of him.

Besides, to him memory has a lot to do with sentiments and Miguel is incapable of feeling affection for someone he has never seen.

"Your real mother also loved you."

"How do you know? She's never told me so."

"She gave you life. Giving someone life is the greatest act of love there can ever be in this world, especially when you lose your own life in the process."

"I don't understand what you're saying."

"You will some day. Hasn't your father explained that your mother in heaven is the one that gave birth to you?"

Miguel withdraws once more. The conversation has taken a turn he doesn't like and what grandfather is saying is too complicated.

"In any case, I'm glad your mother Estrella takes good care of you and loves you."

What happens is that Doctor Gallardo sometimes loses his sense of the present and unconsciously immerses himself in the past, as if time had not passed at all.

So when Miguel explains his version of love and his need to be loved by a mother, he cannot help but imagine Dula as she was the summer they met, when Miguel still did not exist and she, believing herself infertile, felt she had been passed over.

"You can be sure of one thing, Miguel. You and I are going to be good friends, no matter what. I'm going to be with you every minute until your parents come to get you."

"When will they come?"

"At the end of the summer."

"Is that a long time?"

He poses the question anxiously. What Miguel probably needs right now is to believe the wait will be as short as possible. But time is different for children than for adults.

"No Miguel, it isn't very long. You have to remember, though,

43

that summers have days, weeks, and months. But don't worry. Your grandfather is going to do everything he can to make sure you don't miss your parents too much. We'll play together. We'll go out in the boat. We'll fish. And I'll show you all the places where your dad used to hunt for insects and lizards and spiders when he was a little boy just like you."

"Why'd he do that?"

"To take them to his laboratory and analyze them."

"So dad had a snake farm like the Pasteur Institute when he was little?"

"Not exactly. But it was a farm in its own way. And I liked it when he played scientist."

"So do you like snakes too?"

"I've never seen those snake farms, but your parents told me all about them."

Miguel finally relaxes. He is no longer a crybaby. Now he is in the mood to put on airs as if he were very grown up and experienced.

"I have seen them," he announces proudly. "My dad showed them to me. The snakes are kept in very deep, dark pits. They coil up and they fight. And when they take them out to get the venom, you can even touch them."

"You're not going to tell me you've touched them."

The child nods.

"Lots of times. And they never bite me."

"What a brave boy you are. I'm sure the snakes knew that you have guts and if they tried to bite you, you'd have finished them off."

Miguel feels good again. And for the first time since his arrival at Mas Delfín, he can see that everything isn't really so hostile here in this place on the coast and his grandfather can be very nice, even though he is older and his expressions might seem severe.

"My dad told me you write stories."

"That's right. One of these days I might make up a story about you. Would you like that?"

"But I don't know how to read."

"It doesn't matter. You'll learn very soon."

The child hesitates. Then he opens his eyes wide and looks directly at his grandfather.

"One day I'll take you to Bangkok so you can touch a snake."

"Are you sure it won't bite me?"

"It won't because I'll touch it first."

He has declared this firmly, like an adult trying to soothe a child,

44

who is now the grandfather. And as he does so, Dula's features take possession of his face once again.

"You know what, Miguel?" I am so glad to know I have a grandson who is willing to defend me."

Miguel's eyes widen and he becomes increasingly animated.

"Your mom had vivacious eyes just like yours. And, stroking his head, "I don't know if you'll understand what I'm going to say to you, but the truth is, she gave you life and right now you're giving it back to her."

Miguel does not answer. He's not entirely sure whether what his grandfather is saying is good. Besides, it's hard for him to absorb that he could resemble a dead person. But Patricio presses on.

"The color of your eyes and your expressions are just like hers, and even the way you move."

"But how can I look like someone I've never seen?" And before his grandfather can reply, "I want to something to eat. I'm hungry."

Grandfather smiles and hugs him. Hoisting him up on his shoulders, he simulates a trot in the direction of the house, while the child fills the air with peals of laughter.

❊   ❊   ❊

My grandson's arrival has triggered an unexpected pang of conscience, which has stirred up the thousand churning silences I had managed to keep at bay for so long.

But they are back again in all of their infinite detail, resuscitating the sensations, contradictions, and failings of that summer.

Everything seems to be repeating itself. Not only because Miguel is the spitting image of his mother, but because his ups and downs and his unique way of reacting to unexpected situations reminds me of Dula's decline, Gregorio's misgivings, and the interminable struggle that was waged in the culverts of our lives.

Just seeing the two of them together, there on the terrace the night they arrived, Dula's head resting against my son's leg, was enough to observe the deep connection between them. It was palpable in everything. And not just in the exchanged looks, frequent caresses, or the brushing back of a stray lock of hair. It was plain in the compatibility of their ideas, in their conversation.

The way they behaved towards each other was actually quite remarkable. It did not seem as if they'd been married for as long as they had.

45

I remember once, in the middle of a heated conversation, Rodolfo Liaño—always one tell it like it is—took it upon himself to remark easily, "You were right, Gregorio. You're wife is not like other women." And seeing that his comment might have seemed a tad out of place, "Mind you, I don't mean it in any pejorative sense, Dula. I had the same impression the first time I saw your photograph."

Dula responded without hesitation.

"Gregorio is also different. That's why I married him."

I have a feeling that was the day my son first felt something akin to a twinge of alarm. Certain incongruities may be nothing more than reflections of innocuous things that end up changing courses and distorting patterns for no reason at all.

In any event, probably none of what eventually caused Gregorio to detest Liaño would have come to pass had subsequent alarm bells not reinforced his suspicions.

The thing was, those warnings were not really warnings at all, or even causes for concern. But they appeared to be. And that's what turned Liaño into the bad guy in the movie, even though—as Dula and I knew very well—Rodolfo was nothing more than a metaphor created by our own consciences. Whether he knew it or not, he was there to keep the ground under our feet from splitting open and plunging us into the grave of the living dead.

So many July evenings the four of us sat there after dinner was over, conversing and contemplating the sea, with its aroma of dew-dampened forest and sea salts intermingled with the unmistakable scent of violets emanating from my daughter-in-law's body whenever the wind touched her skin.

Paula was not party to our chats at that point. Paula was still the aesthetic rationale behind the sentimental irrationality. But she was not, as yet, trying to monopolize my time and I was not about to let her occupy an important space in my life, if for no other reason than because conversing with Paula was exactly like conversing with Canuto or Leticia. She would never have been able to follow our discussions. And she would have been bored to death, because the only topics she was truly interested came from romance magazines and television programs about the pop scene, daughters of famous mothers, and abandoned women who consoled themselves by shooting their lips fashionably full of silicone in their quest for millionaire husbands.

At first, the conversation almost always flowed around Gregorio and Dula's impassioned work at the Pasteur Institute.

They never tired of discussing the ins and outs of their activities. It left the impression that nothing outside of the ophidian world really interested them. "You should see the snake farm, Dad." And then the intricate description of the wide, deep pits "resembling biblical punishments," which held hundreds of poisonous reptiles. "It's remarkable to look into those pits."

Then they would explain how the Menan river, which bisected the city, was not only home to the Floating Market, but also the principal breeding ground for poisonous animals—reptiles of every sort, Bengal snakes, Russell's vipers, and cobras—"always ready to ambush a human being. You constantly have to be prepared to inject antitoxins."

Then the topic would turn abruptly to my books. Both had read them in depth and they were rigorous in their critiques. Nothing escaped their keen perception and analysis.

It was gratifying to realize my son and his wife had delved so deeply into my writings, examining not only the various techniques I had employed, but also processes, systems, and settings.

"I really liked your description of freedom," Dula told me once. "You're right. No one is free. Whether we like it or not, we are all slaves to something. In fact, true freedom cannot exist without boundaries. It would be impossible to have a river without a channel, the sea without land, life without death and, of course," she continued half-jokingly, "televised broadcasts without television."

And seeing that I just sat their staring at her, mesmerized by her analytical ability, she added, "The essential thing is not to be free. The essential thing is to choose wisely the boundaries that circumscribe our freedom."

How often I have thought back to that evening. Up to then, Dula's voice, unfailingly discreet and gentle, had glided in and out of the conversation, careful never to impose her judgment on the point she was making. That night was different.

That night it was as if she intended to say something that transcended her words. Something akin to a verbal impulse trained to hurdle obstacles and stimulate our thought processes in order to bring them into line with hers.

"So you also believe that no human being can truly feel free?" I asked, watching her intently.

She closed her eyes and breathed deeply.

"The way you describe humanity, Patricio, no one is, in fact, free." And with a trace of a smile, she added, "But there is something which brings us closer to that unattainable freedom."

47

I asked her what that might be and she replied without hesitation.

"At the risk of your laughing at me, I sincerely believe we can only feel truly free when we offer our freedom up to God."

I did not understand her. Her response seemed ambiguous and clichéd. I did not agree with her belief. I had always embraced the notion of a freedom castrated by our human condition.

"Can you really believe there are creatures in this world who consider themselves truly free? Where do you place the greedy, those who act out of their own self-interest, the drug addicts, the jealous, those of us who, one way or another, consider ourselves bound by some vice or habit, some passion or love?"

She nodded with a trace of irony.

"Don't look at me like that, Patricio. I didn't invent this world. I just live in it. But I am convinced that without God, my life could well become a prison cell."

That was our first argument and also the first time we made contact at a metaphysical level, as if we had discovered each other all of a sudden.

It was not long before such points of contact became more frequent. I could not begin to describe their content. They were ephemeral things: phrases or gestures which I cannot recreate in my mind, try as I might, because they were locked away in the past forever.

Still, they were there, in our encounters and sometimes in our partings: instants that left behind a trace of violets and desolation. And in our silences too. Sometimes speaking is what matters least. Sometimes the one thing capable of shaking us up and dislodging our human weakness is precisely that which is not named, not explained, not remarked.

There was, also a verbal connection, which sometimes left Dula unexpectedly vulnerable. Moments in which the two of us, without knowing why, felt compelled to voice our frustrations or our hopes. It would happen without warning, when neither she nor I had sowed any seed that would engender our strange need to confide in the other the small miseries that sometimes beset us in moments of private introspection.

At the time, it did not even occur to us that our confidences—foolish or superfluous as they might be—were the byproduct of a single motivation: to be together, to talk to each other, to comprehend that the only thing that really mattered was knowing we were both there, breathing the same air and contemplating the same view.

Otherwise, nothing we shared was all that important or out of the ordinary. "I would have liked to have been a mother." Or, "You know what, Patricio? I feel the same way Juliana did. The flowers should not be taken from their own special habitats." And, "I must confess, Dula, I get very lonely in the wintertime."

Once Dula mentioned Paula to me.

"It is quite possible that by your side she could turn out to be an important woman."

I remember I burst out laughing. I gazed at her, shaking my head but still grinning.

"There is no hope for Paula, Dula. She is just a decoration."

In this way, a store of meaningless things was gradually forging a bond between us. What we failed to realize was that no matter how trivial the things shared between a man and a woman might be, if the desire to share them becomes a necessity, they can prevail over everything we always believed was essential to us.

The moment arrived, at least for me, when everything revolved around Dula. In reality, I would be hard pressed to describe my urgent need to be with her, to talk with her, to know exactly where she was at any given moment.

More than once, sitting in my study trying to concentrate on the book I had begun, I would be struck by the urge to go out on the balcony in the hopes of glimpsing her in the garden, on the terrace, on the esplanade, or leaning against the railing of the bluff rising up next to the greenhouse.

I realized at some point that Dula visited the greenhouse frequently, particularly at dusk when the flowers seemed about to succumb to their evening slumber. So I, as if propelled by a strange force, would run over there to surprise her. "I happened to notice you coming in here." And together we would regard the extensive variety of flowers and plants that Juliana had meticulously catalogued and Canuto, faithful to her memory, strove to preserve just as meticulously.

Sometimes we would even sit together on the sofa Juliana had installed in the center of the pavilion to make it seem more homey. We'd listen to music and go back to talking about our lives for no other reason than to pronounce the words, hear the other's voice, and note the fluidity of our bodies and with no thought, no awareness whatsoever, of how much this "detached intimacy" was sabotaging us. Gregorio even joined us for some of these botanical visits. He too enjoyed strolling along the floral pathways his mother had laid out with such devotion, stopping before different flowers that attracted his attention. "I like these roses," he'd say. "They have a different scent than the others."

Then we'd play at choosing which flowers were the most resistant, which the prettiest, which the most mysterious. Dula was inclined towards the orchids. "Maybe it's because they have no fragrance." But she was enraptured by the tuberoses, the begonias and the carnations. "Actually geraniums are the most resilient of all." She then launched into one of her humorous comparisons. "Bah, actually geraniums are a lot like sardines. If they were a little less modest and didn't proliferate so much, they'd be more sought after than the orchids. It's all a matter of prestige based on the law of supply and demand."

When Dula let her imagination fly, absolute jewels of humor could come out of her. When this occurred, Gregorio entranced, would turn to me and murmur, "You see, Dad? Dula is special. She's one of a kind."

For his part, Rodolfo rarely brought up my daughter-in-law. When something was gnawing at him, Rodolfo Liaño tended to be sparing with his words, his rancor and his jokes. But he was disturbingly perceptive. Nothing escaped the vigorous grasp of his neurons. He took everything in with the single-minded concentration of the starving. And once he had digested it all, he would cautiously ponder what he should do, or say, or not say.

Therefore, when he came into my study that afternoon with the air of someone all pent up inside, I knew it would not be long before he said something I was not going to like.

"Please excuse me, Patricio, but I feel I must speak with you."

I don't know why, but I knew immediately what he was going to say. As we settled ourselves on the sofa next to the fireplace and he cleared his throat, I was already thinking about how I was going to respond, just how frank I should be with him, whether I should allow the truth I was trying to hide—had not even dared to admit to myself—to be aired between us.

I offered him a drink, but he demurred.

"It's important to have a clear mind."

Then he spoke frankly to me about Dula.

"Something is weighing on your daughter-in-law, Patricio. I suppose you've already noticed."

No, I had not noticed that Dula was no longer the same person who had left Thailand to visit Mas Delfín. Not for an instant did I imagine my son's wife as someone who felt her self slipping away, someone who was casting about for her lost essence. I only knew—or thought I knew—that I was absolutely necessary to her too. A father figure or mentor, perhaps, who understood her, admired her, and who sometimes enjoyed sitting by her side just to contemplate her features, hear her voice, and allow her violet scent to impregnate my senses.

"Dula has misplaced her joy, Patricio. And worse yet, Gregorio is beginning to realize she isn't the same anymore."

No matter what, I still refused to let him twist my arm.

"It must be just a passing cloud. When she gets back to Thailand, everything will return to normal."

But Rodolfo Liaño wasn't about to let me feign ignorance. Rodolfo Liaño knows me too well to pretend to go along with my pretense.

"Let's be frank, Patricio. It is possible you haven't noticed that Dula has changed, but you're not going to deny to my face that the two of you are moving dangerously close to the snake pit."

I did not answer him. There was no way to refute what he was saying and it would have been ludicrous to get angry or act offended. No matter how much Dula and I had tried to filter the truth of our encounters, our shared confidences, and the sense of wellbeing we felt when we were together, something akin to a dangerous spell was propelling us towards an abyss from which there was no return.

"We're talking about your son, Patricio. Remember that."

Then he left. Left me there with my truth raw and exposed, my deceptions shattered.

Rodolfo was right and it would have been insane to deny it. That very afternoon, therefore, everything changed between Dula and me. There was no more surprising her in the greenhouse or confiding my diatribes against Paula, or listening to confidences, large or small, spill from her lips about her frustration at not having a child or her sadness at the thought of returning to Thailand at the end of the summer.

In reality, it was all over. Because from then on Mas Delfín stopped being what it was before and became a minefield where I was constantly obliged to watch every step I took.

Especially when one morning, while Dula and Liaño were enjoying a boat ride around the bay, Gregorio, an edge to his voice and trace of anguish in his expression, gave me to understand that things between him and Dula were not working as they had before.

"I don't know what's wrong, Dad, but Dula isn't the same."

I regarded him impassively, as if I had no idea what he was trying to tell me.

"I wonder if I am doing something wrong, Dad. I'm confused. Please help me figure out what's happening to me."

God, at that moment I was nothing but a raw abscess of shame inside. I felt a stabbing pain at my son's suffering, and a sense of impotence because I could not hug him like when he was little. There was no way to console him, to repeat a thousand times over that I loved him, that he should forgive me, and that I'd do everything in my power not to interfere with his life, to keep it from being destroyed.

But all I said was, "Come on, Gregorio, don't be so hard on yourself. Stop imagining things. Women are temperamental creatures, Son. Even your mother, perfect as she was, would go all berserk with the phases of the moon. And yet she always loved me. I am as sure of her love as I am of the love Dula professes for you."

❋   ❋   ❋

Paula, meanwhile, was busy planning the imminent grand opening of the Verde Mar Hotel.

It promised to be a momentous occasion. After all, it was a luxury hotel and in addition to the private invitations extended to coastal residents, a number of celebrities, politicians, and government officials had been invited.

Besides, according to Paula, there was going to be music, folkloric dancing and famous comedians, and naturally, journalists, columnists from romance magazines, and private and public television would be in attendance.

I had received several calls from the hotel director entreating me to be sure to attend and of course to bring my family and anyone else who happened to be staying at Mas Delfín at the time.

On the night of the grand event, Paula had sheathed herself in a red gown that caught the eye even from a distance. The contrast with her tanned skin and blond mane accentuated the fabulous physique beneath the silky cloth that clung to her body, leaving most of her breasts and long legs exposed.

Paula certainly did attract looks like a magnet. She was so striking she cast a pall over the potential charms of the other women present.

Even Rodolfo Liaño was dazzled when he caught sight of her that evening. "What a woman," he told me. "I can see why you would be infatuated with her."

But Paula really was all looks: an astonishing visual offering composed strictly of physical perfections. Nonetheless, I would by lying if I did not admit I was flattered by the sensation she caused that evening, particularly among the men.

It is sobering to realize, in hindsight, just how foolish a man can be when he allows his actions to be dictated by a narcissistic desire to be envied for something as stupid as having been chosen by a girl who has virtually nothing to recommend her aside from her physical charms.

And yet that evening, I, Patricio Gallardo, renowned writer and physician by profession, was just another poor bastard who melted—or pretended to melt—for a woman who quickly became nothing more than an illusion. A valueless object which is still there simply because I have not yet bothered to implore her to get out of my life.

It was, admittedly, an evening of vegetable impulses and powerful epidermic sensations. And it is even possible that my behavior was due not only to the alcohol ingested or the fear of stepping on mines that could injure my son. It is quite likely that—apart from my eagerness to stay away from Dula, as Liaño had advised—I also was attracted to Paula. So it was not such a hardship after all to use her as an excuse to keep my distance from Dula.

It was a tense evening. An evening during which the important thing was to be with Paula, to speak with Paula, to recreate the view around the spectacle Paula presented.

Intoxicated by the excitement I was experiencing—probably artificial and certainly impulsive—I remember begging Paula to become part of the family atmosphere at Mas Delfín from that night on, whenever her work schedule allowed. "You can join us anytime you like. You'll always be welcome."

Paula was grateful. She found it hard to believe a man regarded as an important intellectual would notice a woman like her, greatly admired for her physical attributes but not for her nonexistent metaphysical ones.

I hardly saw Dula that evening. In fact, my plan had been not to see her, or speak to her, or even think about her. It was the right thing to do. It would rapidly neutralize the absurd desire to be together at every opportunity for the sole purpose of sharing increasingly dangerous confidences.

Unassuming by nature, Dula was adept at absenting herself without anyone having to tell her to do so. Therefore, my demeanor alone would have sufficed for her to adopt a similar posture. It was the best thing we could do. Everything becomes easier when one's private intentions are reinforced by the conduct of others. That evening, Dula must have discerned right away how much I desired her collaboration. We never spoke of it, but it was as if we had made a pact with no paper, no words, no spoken pledges, yet as binding as any legal agreement.

There was just one moment when this false euphoria of mine very nearly collapsed. It was when, dancing with Paula, I abruptly bumped into my son dancing with his wife.

I remember Gregorio regarding me with a slightly sardonic smile. I am sure he too was affected by my magnificent partner. He turned suddenly and Dula and I were face to face. She gazed at me wordlessly, her eyes glistening, and her lips—with a trace of lipstick—suggested not a smile, but something more akin to sadness. Then her gaze drifted away, as if hoping to lose itself in who knew what strange sorrows.

That night, I stayed at the Verde Mar Hotel. I have no idea what time Liaño, Gregorio, and she left. All I know is that when I returned to Mas Delfín around noon, the three of them were already down at the beach, awaiting my return.

The first one to toss a sarcastic comment my way was my son, Gregorio. "So it looks as if things are serious with Paula, Dad." He chuckled. "You know you're about to commit infanticide, don't you?" he said. And still grinning, "Who would have thought it? My father, in love with a mere slip of a girl."

Even Liaño joined in the teasing. "I agree. You've always said reason must prevail over emotions in a writer, but damn, literature aside, you have to admit you upended your own principles last night." He said it aloud so the others could hear him.

Dula did not comment. She merely contemplated the sea as if her husband's and Rodolfo's banter was of no interest to her.

From that day forward, Paula, feeling herself on more solid footing, showed up at Mas Delfín whenever she was able to extricate from the Verde Mar Hotel. And if she wasn't able to get away, I would go over there.

The issue was to avoid at all cost the illness that had gradually compelled me to turn to Dula. And Paula was pain-relief medicine.

I would frequently tell the kids, "I'm sorry but I won't be having dinner with you this evening." Gregorio and Rodolfo would exchange complicit looks. They both knew perfectly well that the "won't be having dinner" meant I had a date with Paula. But they merely smiled. "It's really just as if you were having dinner with a sister of mine," joked Gregorio.

Again, Dula would remain silent. But if Gregorio's and Rodolfo's jokes intensified, she did not hesitate to intervene, "Well, your father is a widower. He has a right to enjoy himself." Her voice was cutting, with an edge of controlled anger, as if she genuinely felt it her duty to defend her father-in-law. And I was grateful to her because deep down—and though she never would have confessed this to me—I knew my trysts with Paula hurt her just as they soon would begin to hurt me.

I often call to mind those July days, trying to figure out what really caused me to tire so easily of my new conquest.

The truth is, my sudden enthusiasm vanished as quickly as it had arrived. It was probably her voice that most contributed to my waning interest in her. No body, no matter how perfect, can make up for the continuous assault of a shrill, whiny voice. At least I've never been able to abide it.

Then to discover that what the voice discharged was an affront, not only to good sense, but to even a modicum of common sense.

The bad thing about Paula was, besides not knowing how to speak, she also did not know how to listen. While she had mastered the art of moving, looking, and insinuating, she was incapable of maintaining any semblance of a decent conversation.

Then there was her accent: coarse, strident, sing-song. It had driven me crazy from the outset.

I soon learned that it was one thing to be with her in bed and quite another to be with her in any situation where reason would dictate a modicum of intellectual decorum or a reasonably acceptable appearance.

In sum, Paula was the proverbial bunch of green grapes the fox could not reach. And the worse part was, she hadn't a clue.

It was no use to try to correct her. "But you understood me, right?" she'd retort with a self-assured air. "So why the hell do I have to talk like you do?"

Sometimes, just to please me, she'd grab onto one of my books and rush right through it like those misguided readers who want only to get to the end. When she was finished she would invariably say she liked it a lot, except that half of what I wrote was unintelligible. "I don't get what you mean when . . ." She reproached me for what she referred to as "such complicated plots." To Paula's way of thinking, the most important thing about a novel was whether you liked reading the story and most importantly, whether it had a "happy ending."

"I really don't get your obsession with giving your novels such unpleasant endings."

No use trying to explain to her that in life, there are no endings. Until we die, everything that happens is just a series of precarious, free-floating circumstances awaiting the real ending, which is death.

"Nothing is stable Paula. Everything is subject to change from one day to the next."

"Everything?"

"Everything."

"Even your feelings towards me?"

I hesitated a few seconds before responding. I was moved by her expression: half innocent, half idiotic.

"Relax, Paula. What I feel for you isn't going to change."

I wasn't lying. It already had changed.

Soon after, Liaño returned to my study to speak with me again.

"I'm up to here with Paula," I said in a burst of sincerity.

Rodolfo stared at the floor for a good while.

"In any case, it has been an effective catalyst to keep you away from Dula," he said finally.

I'd already figured that out, but I did not reply.

"It's a shame Paula hasn't been able to rise to the occasion," continued Rodolfo. "But if I may say so, Patricio, at your age you really should focus on women more in your league.

He was right, but I didn't want to admit it to him.

"I've always told you it would be hard to find another Juliana."

Rodolfo shook his head, as if to say he was not persuaded by my argument.

"Gregorio has found her," he said.

And he left the room.

The truth is, I used the same excuses that initially had served to bring me closer to Paula to distance myself from her. "I'm neglecting the kids, Paula. I can't see you tonight." Or, "It would be better if you didn't come to Mas Delfín at our regular beach time tomorrow. I've promised to take the kids fishing."

And she took it. "Okay, I'll wait for you to call."

I have to acknowledge it: despite everything, Paula was not a demanding or unaccommodating woman.

She soon became something like a slave to me. She probably intuited that I would leave her if she ever confronted me. No doubt she believed our relationship was simply a matter of time, of being patient and waiting it out. A matter of letting out some line and reeling it in at the right moment to ensure we would always be together.

And truth be told, she has succeeded up to now. Dula is dead, and she is still here.

* * *

The night was calm and Miguel has slept peacefully well into the morning. Doctor Gallardo himself has gone to his room to wake him. "The child needs to get accustomed to European time."

Before waking the child, however, Patricio pauses for a moment by the bed to look at him.

There is his grandson, still sound asleep, his face flushed, eyes closed, sweaty blond hair clinging to his temples and forehead, his mouth half-open.

"Miguel."

But Miguel does not move. He's probably dreaming because he suddenly makes a face that could easily be a smile or a pout.

Maybe he imagines he's still traveling among wandering clouds that some child Morpheus is creating just for him. Surely he has no idea he is no longer in Bangkok, is actually lying in the bed that belonged to his father when he was a little boy.

It is touching to see him sleeping so peacefully, so oblivious to his surroundings. It's also a little frightening to imagine what lies in store for that face, with its diminutive features and soft skin, when it becomes the face of a man.

No one can know, in a given moment, what type of life lies ahead, what problems will beset one, what passions might compel one to throw principles to the wind, what impossible promises will be left dangling.

Doctor Gallardo is recalling something Dula said when he tried to lift her spirits about her presumed infertility. "You're right, Patricio. A child is like a box, empty of matter but full of unknowns. That's why, even though I am frustrated, I'm sometimes glad I'm sterile."

To the child, Patricio thinks now, the world around him is just a murmur or a vague outline. The bad thing is when the murmur turns into a roar or the outline into a picture.

The day they had spoken of infertility, they were sitting on the beach observing Liaño and Gregorio try to keep an unexpected gust from releasing the boats from their moorings.

"Wake up, Miguel," whispers the grandfather, kissing him.

Feeling the kiss brush his face, Miguel opens his eyes. Then he frowns and looks about him, confused and not entirely sure where he is.

"Good morning," his grandfather says again.

The child reacts. He recognizes his grandfather but is still not quite able to figure out what he is doing in a strange bedroom.

"You must be hungry. It's very late."

The child regards him wide-eyed.

"And my parents? Where are my parents?"

"Don't you remember? They've gone to Brazil."

"And what about me? What am I going to do?"

"Now you're going to have your breakfast. Then we'll go down to the beach. Do you know how to swim?"

"Of course I know how to swim."

"Well then, jump out of bed."

Standing, he leans down to kiss him one more time.

Miguel smells clean, like soap, despite the sweat. Leticia probably bathed him last night before putting him to bed. His forehead is cool. It is the coolness of healthy skin, of bodies able to withstand the onslaught of adversity with no ill effects.

Still, the grandfather thinks again, life will start to replace the coolness of that skin with the heat of the struggle, of races against time, the desire to come out on top along with the shame of not achieving it, or else distrust toward the successful, the constant wondering whether someone is waiting to trip one up.

Later he will also learn to love and perhaps to hate. And to need presences and to feel as if he were dying should the absences turn out to be forever.

"Dad wants me to say my prayers before I get up."

Patricio had already forgotten that particular instruction.

"You're right, Miguel. You should obey your father."

"Where should I start?"

Patricio has no idea. Patricio has neglected his discourse with God for some time now.

"I'll call Leticia. She can help you."

But Leticia appears immediately. Patricio did not even have to call her.

"How did my boy sleep?"

There she goes with her "my boy" again, thinks Miguel. He is not her boy. And he is not his grandfather's boy either.

"I have to say my prayers," he insists. "Dad wants me to say my prayers."

Dula had also been devout. Patricio is seeing her now, entering the local church and advancing slowly towards the altar, her eyes downcast, hands clasped. Her desire to remain unnoticed is palpable, breaking the parishioners' concentration, because one look at her was enough to make everything else fade into the background.

It was one afternoon after Sunday mass when Dula, out of curiosity, had asked him why he hadn't taken communion like everyone else. "I'm not in a position to do so," he responded. She suddenly realized her indiscretion. "I'm sorry. I shouldn't have meddled in something so private."

By then Dula's vivacity had already begun to fade. She no longer said thought-provoking things, or retorted with some peculiar aphorism, or tossed out perplexing questions as she used to.

And when her father-in-law tried to coax out of her the reasons for the change, all she said was, "there is no room for tactlessness in this life." And she quickly added, "I need to be more careful about what I say."

She clearly was referring to the question she had put to her father-in-law after Sunday mass. She seemed to feel as if she had to make it up to him, because she spent the rest of the day in a state of self-mortification over the blessed indiscretion. It was as if she had to punish herself for having committed an inexcusable transgression.

Recalling now his reaction when he observed her distress. "I also tend to be tactless, and thickheaded, and of course, fickle. You see, Dula, I consider myself a Catholic yet all my life I've behaved as if I am not one. Is there anything more tactless than professing to be a believer yet behaving like an atheist?"

She laughed when her father-in-law said that. "We should all learn a lesson from snakes, you know that, Patricio? They teach us to be prudent. Remember the saying, "be then, prudent as the serpents, and guileless as the doves?"

Now Miguel is also muttering something about doves. It is a prayer Leticia has come up with referring to the purity of the soul. The child is repeating after Leticia. He probably does not understand most of what he is saying since his parents taught him different prayers. But he follows along because he does not know how to convince this woman that her prayers aren't like the ones he's used to saying.

When he finishes, he turns to his grandfather and shoots from the cuff.

"Is it true that, besides writing, you also know how to tell stories?"

"Of course it is."

"Well tonight when I go to bed, I want you to tell me one. But not the same old ones."

"And what are the same old ones?"

"You know. Little Red Riding Hood or Snow White or Cinderella. Those are for girls. I like stories about extraterrestrial monsters, murderers, and robbers."

"Good stories or bad stories?"

Miguel shrugs.

"I don't know. I just want them to be exciting."

Now Patricio wonders what Dula would think about what her child has just said: "I just want them to be exciting." Which is the state of being of a child, a child's hopes, and a child's truth. And this was the world he was offering him. A world devoid of ethics. A world capable of experiencing emotions but incapable of channeling them. An un-settled world, with no roads, no signposts, no directions to indicate the way out of the un-settlement.

"Good stories can be exciting too."

"Okay, so tell me a good story."

"A true story?"

"Sure, a true story."

Doctor Gallardo wonders wherein lies the truth of his life. Indeed, living for him has been like crossing a vast, barren plateau fraught with bewildering signals.

That's what it had felt like, at least, that afternoon when Dula, after apologizing for her tactlessness, had implored him to forget what she had asked him about communion. "You needn't worry," he had told her. "All you have done is voice what your common sense dictates to you. Sensible people like you cannot fail to notice the contradictions. And my truth—why deny it?—is very inconsistent." And after a prolonged silence, "Fortunately, your husband is nothing like me. He takes after his mother."

The wind picked up and it was getting chilly on the beach. But before getting up, Patricio had turned to her smiling, "actually, you're a lot like Juliana too."

The sea was taking on a leaden tone that augured a storm. The cirrus clouds of the preceding day had disappeared and the sky was darkening into angry shades. "We should get back to the house. It's going to start pouring any minute." Liaño and Gregorio were signaling for them to go on ahead. "We're almost finished tying up the boats."

They quickened their step at the first rumble of thunder. It was a strange afternoon. Everything around them had suddenly turned hostile.

The slope from the beach up to the esplanade and the house is somewhat steep and sometimes, when you speed up, the heart will beat a little too quickly.

He recalls now that Dula was beside him, wordlessly trying to keep up. They stopped abruptly. "We're almost there," he said, and they continued up to the terrace. Just then it began to rain. "What a coincidence. The rain waited until we were safely under cover." And despite her lethargic expression, she attempted to smile. "Hasn't anyone ever told you that coincidences are merely destinies traveling incognito?"

It was impossible to know what she was referring to. It could be the rain, or the glowering sky, or the confusion that had taken hold of them both.

Suddenly, as if propelled by the same spring, they headed for the house. Leticia came out to meet them "You've arrived just in time," she said. "It's about to pour down rain." But Dula did not answer. She ran for the stairs without explanation and shut herself in her room. She did not come out again until her husband had returned.

* * *

Suddenly, the phone.

"Miss Paula is calling."

Patricio took the receiver.

"I wanted to know whether the child arrived okay."

"Just fine, thank you."

And quickly, "I know you don't need me Patricio, but if you want me to, I have no problem helping you put up with him."

"It's not a matter of putting up with him, Paula. I enjoy spending time with my grandson. He's a funny, unique, and bright little boy."

"But we women are naturally better equipped to care for children than you are."

Sometimes Paula can be incredibly interfering. She does not know how to gauge how far she can go when it comes to Patricio's likes and dislikes. And she's irritating. Especially when, convinced of her entitlements as the lady of Mas Delfín, she takes it upon herself to remind Patricio of certain scenes from the summer Doctor Gallardo is anxious to forget. "Remember your daughter-in-law's face the first time you showed her the greenhouse? She was so clueless she thought the missing flowers should never have been sacrificed just to fill some vases. Why would the flowers be in that god-forsaken building in the first place, if not to decorate the house?" Or else, "I always said your daughter-in-law was a little strange. For one thing, she didn't like it when I went into the kitchen to give Leticia her instructions. Or maybe she thought *she* was the lady of the house?"

"I'm telling you once and for all, I don't need you, Paula."

"So you don't want to see me?"

"It would be better if we saw each other after Miguel leaves."

Paula's voice is suddenly plaintive.

"Fine then. I'll wait until the little boy leaves. Anything in order not to ruin our relationship."

"Please don't be so melodramatic."

And cheerful again, "I was just kidding. You know I would never leave you."

"I don't doubt it, Paula. In any event, maybe I'll call you sometime."

"I'll wait for you."

The good thing about Paula is she never gets mad. She does not make demands or impose ultimatums.

"And don't worry, Patricio. I don't want to be a bother to you."

Replacing the receiver, Doctor Gallardo turns to his grandson.

"Get ready, because we're going down to the beach now. We'll fish and swim and do whatever you like. Does that sound good?"

"Okay."

He also proposes taking him to the town in the afternoon to buy ice cream, visit the toy stores, and do whatever it is Miguel likes to do.

"Could you buy me a costume?"

"Whatever you like."

"A Superman costume?"

"And the Power Rangers, and the Three Musketeers. Anything you want."

The child smiles. And to Patricio, his smile is like a thousand butterflies taking wing. Later he begins to prance impatiently from one end of the terrace to the other like a restless puppy anxious to thank his owner for giving him so many treats.

He stops all of a sudden.

"What are you thinking about, grandfather?"

"About the greenhouse."

He points to the building, now quite old, adjacent to the rising bluff.

"I'd like to see it."

"I don't think so. There's nothing there but flowers and plants."

"I know. Canuto told me. He also told me that flowers have souls."

"That's what your grandmother believed."

The child frowns, hesitates, and then regards him curiously.

"Where is my grandmother now?"

Patricio squats down to the child's level. He strokes his face.

"She is with your mother."

"Which one?"

"The one that didn't go to Brazil."

Miguel's mood shifts suddenly. He feels uncomfortable. He must have decided this grandmother is not going to be of much use to him either. She has vanished into the air and into the silences, just as his mother, Dula, did.

"So, nothing."

"No matter what, I can assure you that your grandmother loves you very much."

"How do you know?"

Children are definitely capable of persecuting adults with their questions, backing them into corners from which it is hard to see a way out.

"After all, you are her son's son."

"And that's enough for her to love me?"

Here we go again. This unexpected, volatile, and strange relationship does not fit into the child's understanding of things, but he only nods and does not admit that he cannot comprehend any of it.

"So I have to love her too?"

And here again, how can you love something or someone that cannot be seen, does not move, and makes no sound?

"Just be good. That will make her very happy."

And with that, he grabs the child around the waist and hoists him over his head and onto his shoulders.

"Shall we go?"

"Let's go."

And they wend their way down the path to the beach.

The two are happy, singing made-up songs that the grandfather tries to apply to the child.

"The sun awaits the grandfather, the sea awaits Miguel. The sky watches over them both, covering them with her veil."

"Again."

The tune stays the same, but the words keep changing because the grandfather keeps forgetting what he has just made up.

But it doesn't matter. Although the words are indecipherable, the child understands them. He knows exactly what his grandfather is telling him with each inflection, each word.

"Here we are."

And there is the beach. A little unkempt, because the tourists discovered this hidden nook a while back and have taken it upon themselves to divest it of its status as a little hideaway tucked out of sight and forgotten by nature.

Now, Mas Delfín's little beach bears no resemblance to the beach Dula knew six years ago. Canuto is still there, however, getting the boat and the fishing gear ready.

The day is calm, perfect for a trip along the coast.

"Will there be some fish?"

"If there are, we will fish them out."

"Can we eat them?"

"Of course."

Once they are in the boat, Canuto gives it a push off the beach. The boy is seated in the stern and the grandfather on the bench, rowing with the same vigor as before, when Dula would ensconce herself just where her child is now seated.

"Why are you looking at me like that, Grandfather?"

"I wasn't looking at you. I was looking at your mother."

Something tells Miguel that his grandfather is not talking about Estrella, but about the other one. He does not reply.

"She smelled of violets."

As he speaks, Patricio can see Dula jumping off the boat into the water. "Don't follow me, Patricio. I'll swim back to the beach."

"Why did she smell like violets?"

"I guess she liked that kind of perfume."

"Well, what do I smell like?"

"A blond boy with black eyes."

On that other day, Dula was already gone when Patricio returned

64

to the beach. She'd gone into the city with Rodolfo Liaño to pick up her husband, who was returning from a meeting of physicians in Madrid.

Doctor Gallardo seems to recall that as the same night Rodolfo spoke with him again about Dula, with a certain edge to his voice. "She's been acting like a wayward soul for days now. You must have noticed."

But he could only think of the void she would leave behind in Mas Delfín when she returned to Thailand. "Let's hope it all changes when she leaves." But Rodolfo did not concur. "Don't delude yourself, Patricio. Certain wounds never heal. And you know why? Because the imprints of those who caused them refuse to be erased."

※　※　※

In spite of everything, I often imagine that if Dula and Gregorio had left earlier, instead of staying at Mas Delfín until the end of September, the strange attraction we had to struggle to ignore would have vanished into time and space just as if there had never been any other sort of attraction between us than that of a father and a daughter.

But they stayed. And our efforts to make everything appear normal slowly mutated into something akin to a conspiracy between Liaño, Dula, and me, to keep Gregorio from glimpsing the vague silhouette of misery that was transforming our lives into an inferno.

Indeed, although we never admitted it even to ourselves or made any attempt to plan how we would act, the conspiracy was there. It was futile to try to deny it. Our lives were gradually being sucked into a labyrinth and when the way out was discovered, one of the three was bound to be affected one way or another. Complicities—even when unplanned or unanticipated in a rational sense—are always found out, and sometimes it is the innocent accomplice who gets hurt.

Which is exactly what happened to Rodolfo Liaño a few days later. But in early July, Gregorio still regarded Rodolfo as the highly efficient man who managed to deploy his usefulness as subtly as possible to ensure that everything at Mas Delfín functioned as it should.

But the rebus was there on the table—a jumble of dreams, illusions, fears, dissimulation, and silences—and none of us dared to assemble the pieces.

Around that time, Gregorio proposed we bicycle into town on the path. "Like when I was little, remember Dad?"

When we arrived, we parked the bikes by the fountain to one side of the square. Everything was still normal between us. Gregorio and Dula had just arrived at Mas Delfín a few days before and there was as yet no sign of the covert impulses we were compelled to bury one by one as the summer wore on.

A lot was happening in town that day. The tourists were flocking to the coast and the beaches had already been transformed into the noisy chaos that naked sun and water lovers tend to produce as they air out the winter's oppression with shouting matches, infantile games, and unbridled foolishness.

I remember that the air was clear and the sun, although still blazing, was gradually retreating towards Daní mountain, as slightly confused cicadas launched into their evening symphony, apparently forgetting that July days are the longest of all.

The view of the town from the central square never fails to amaze. I was therefore not surprised at Dula's look of astonishment when we arrived. "My God, how beautiful."

The panorama had left her speechless. The eye was called in every direction: towards clusters of white houses and narrow streets snaking upward under lopsided arches dating back to medieval times, or the strip of shops built on the edge of town in order to leave the architectural design of the old sector intact.

That afternoon, as Gregorio was describing the intricacies of everything around us, he thought to mention the hermitage on Daní mountain. "There is a saint who performs miracles in the hermitage." At least that was its fame among the townspeople. They called him, "the saint of the fishermen" and more than one claimed to have been saved from death in the middle of a storm by his divine intervention. Dula tried unsuccessfully to find out his name. No one knew it. "It doesn't matter what his name is. The important thing is that he's a saint who performs miracles," they told her.

No, that day Dula was not dragging around the desperate lassitude that so upset my son, which she tried to suppress with smiles that made her look as if she were on the verge of tears.

That afternoon at least, her excitement was obvious and her devotion to Gregorio as strong as the day of their arrival at Mas Delfín.

I remember how, with little explanation, she grabbed her husband by the hand and begged him to explore the town with her. "I want to examine every nook and cranny with you." And turning to Rodolfo and me. "We'll meet you here later, by the fountain."

It was an unanticipated escape that left us at loose ends for the afternoon. "I must confess your daughter-in-law baffles me," Rodolfo said, as he watched the couple make their way towards the hidden streets. "They're happy," I responded. "Sometimes young people need to let themselves be carried away. They have a right to take off and revel in their happiness however they like."

They took their time coming back. When they finally arrived, they were flushed and out of breath, their eyes shining. "I wouldn't mind living in this town forever," I can recall Dula saying.

I watched her walk with a mysterious air towards the water flowing from the fountain's spout. She was radiant, her eyes wide, her movements reminiscent of the dancers from her homeland. She put her ear up against the stream of water that flowed into the basin. "Did you know? Every fountain makes a different sound. Each one composes its own unique melody."

Once again, Liaño's confusion, Gregorio's look of utter enchantment, and my astonishment. For an instant it was as if Juliana were there, assuring me that flowers do indeed have souls. The metaphors were essentially the same.

"What sort of melodies?" I inquired, half joking. Dula turned towards me tensing slightly. "If you can't hear it yourself, you'll never know, Patricio. It's intuitive."

That night we did not go out onto the terrace after dinner. The sky had clouded over again and the wind rushing in across the sea sent the waves crashing onto the shore, filling the air with humidity and the tang of seawater.

Despite the darkness, it was possible to make out the lights of vessels heading towards land to avoid the impending storm.

"A sure sign that bad weather is on the way," Gregorio said. Indeed, it always stormed when the preceding days had been warm and benevolent.

That was also the evening we talked about snakes. Gregorio assured us there were curative poisons and that in the old days, people knew a lot more about natural remedies. "As a matter of fact, the Chinese were pioneers in the study of the human body." Dula remained silent. At times she gave the impression she was not there at all, was not aware of what her husband was saying. Twice I caught her watching me out of the corner of her eye. But she immediately turned back to Gregorio, huddling against his legs and stroking his calf as she always did.

Suddenly, out of the blue she said something that took us all aback. "Life can be very short. We shouldn't waste it searching all over the place for crumbs when the real food is within our grasp. I supposed she was referring to what Gregorio had said about the medical achievements of the Chinese. But that night, after we had gone upstairs and were alone in my study, Liaño pinioned me with a worried expression. "What were you thinking when Dula said that?"

I answered him truthfully. "In the huge hole the kids are going to leave behind when they go."

"That's still a long way off," he responded. And later, as if after much thought, he added, "sometimes absences are like leeches on the soul."

I suddenly realized that Rodolfo was right. Dula was too vital to be forgotten. "I can see why my son is fascinated by her."

The truth is, from that day forward, in our desire to keep the couple from taking off and leaving us alone, Rodolfo and I dreamed up a thousand plans to keep them at home.

I invited our closest neighbors from along the coast. I organized bridge games and boat trips to remote areas so Dula could discover the rocky passageways to which I had always been drawn because of their mythological atmosphere and the legends of what was supposed to have taken place there.

"I wonder what these rocks would have witnessed a thousand years ago," she said on one occasion. Whatever it was—attacks, shipwrecks, heroic acts, tragedies or loves—it was all lost, just like the priceless treasures that sink to the bottom of the sea never to be discovered.

3

The fishing was good that first day and ever since, Miguel has been determined to take the boat out every morning and drag the ocean floor in search of those slippery nervous creatures that swish furiously away to avoid being trapped by human hands.

But today his grandfather has a different plan.

"We'll go into town. I want you to have a chance to go on the rides they've set up in the square. Do you know what a merry-go-round is?"

"No."

"Don't worry. You'll like it."

Miguel agrees. Even though he's been at Mas Delfín for several days now, his grandfather hasn't let him down once, so he's sure he can count on him.

"So we'll go into town?"

"Yes we will. This is the first day of our big town festival, the 'Fiesta Mayor'."

"What is that?"

Whatever it is, Miguel likes the sound of the word "fiesta." It sounds like fun, like playing, as if it's anything but boring. But he still doesn't know what it means.

"Come on, Grandfather, tell me what it is."

"First imagine the whole town on holiday."

"You're not tricking me are you?"

He recalls now how Gregorio was so wary of being tricked when he was little. "Grown-ups tell a lot of lies."

"I have never tricked a child."

"Never?"

"Never."

While the answer appeases him, he is still not totally convinced. Miguel firmly believes, as did his father before him, that grown-ups have a tendency to lie when they are talking to children. And their lies are so blatant that when Miguel detects one, you can see the blood rush to his face.

He pulls himself up abruptly, brazenly, and crossing his arms with a severe expression, he faces the liar with an offended look. Particularly when the offending party is Leticia. "So here we have Mr. Proper," she is fond of saying when Miguel gets angry.

But it has been several days now since Miguel has gotten angry. His solid pact with his grandfather precludes it. Patricio seems more like another kid than a grandfather. Someone who tries to understand his reactions, whims, and feelings, who relates to him at his level, and makes sure he is happy.

Another thing he likes about grandfather is how self-assured he is in times of danger. Especially when the sky becomes angry, and the sea turns into a huge pus-filled ditch, and thunder pounds the ground with the force of a drill.

"Come here little fellow. I'll protect you."

And there are times when the fears just can't be avoided. Silly little things can bring them on. For example, when Canuto starts to yell.

"Why does he yell like that?"

And Patricio invents an answer to explain Canuto's yells.

"He doesn't like it when people step on the plants in his garden."

"He also keeps repeating a strange thing: 'Eye-chit-in-the-milk.' What does that mean, Grandfather?"

"He's saying 'I'd like some milk.' He's just asking Leticia to get him some milk."

"Canuto's favorite thing is to go in the greenhouse. He says grandmother comes back to life there. Especially if he puts on a record."

"Your grandmother loved flowers."

"Do you?"

"I don't know. I used to like them."

"And now?"

How to explain to him that the greenhouse is sometimes the most beautiful deception of his life, while at other times it is, to him, a living hell?

"Right now I'd be happy if a huge wave came and swept it away."

"How come you've never shown it to me?"

"There's plenty of time. I promise I'll show it to you one day."

Miguel does not protest. Every time he brings it up something happens to grandfather he does not like. It's as if a cloud of sadness passes over his face.

Probably, the child thinks now, grandfather is afraid to go in there and find grandmother's body. But he quickly changes his mind. Grandfather is brave. He's never afraid of anything.

Which is why, in the dark hours before dawn when Miguel is assailed by nighttime fears he cannot suppress, he jumps out of bed and runs to the safety of Patricio's room. "Please Grandfather, let me sleep with you." And he quickly climbs into bed to calm down.

It's basically the same as when Gregorio tucked him in like he used to do in Bangkok.

Miguel likes nothing better than to cuddle up against the big, strong man and feel the warmth of his arm under his neck. "Can you rub my head, Grandfather?" Which actually consisted of running his hand over the child's forehead, head, and back until he fell fast asleep.

Waking up was always fun. They would immediately start planning the day's activities. "I'll take you into the woods to hunt butterflies." Or "soon we'll start organizing your birthday party. Remind me to tell Liaño." Or "we'll rent a bicycle and I'll show you how to ride it on the path, just like I taught your father." Patricio never ran out of ideas to make the child feel lucky and not miss his parents too much.

So far Miguel's favorite activity has been going out to sea to fish. When the sun's rays were less scorching and the still waters allowed one to glimpse their deepest secrets through the glass on the bottom of the boat, Miguel and Patricio could spend hours in the middle of the bay tossing nets or fishing hooks into the sea until their basket was filled with fish "for Leticia to cook that very night."

But he was curious about the Fiesta Mayor.

"So what happens at the Fiesta Mayor?"

"A lot of things happen. People dress up in their Sunday best. The buildings are lighted up and you hear music everywhere, and they set up all the rides so the children can have fun."

And as he speaks, Patricio recalls the Fiesta Mayor of that other summer. Dula had never been to such a spectacle. "These festivals are typical on the coast," her husband explained.

Paula had joined them that year. She had been radiant in her pink dress, her blonde mane undulating down her back.

The atmosphere was still relaxed. There had been nothing save a few momentary lapses that were barely noticeable: an unexpected brushing up against, perhaps, or a breath warming the neck when, for example, they were playing bridge and Dula approached to observe their hands. Then too, a renegade glance might have slipped past with no thought of being discovered. But these were minor things. Minute, unplanned gestures that could never hurt anyone.

"And when will we go to the Fiesta Mayor, Grandfather?"

"When the sun goes down. It is still very hot."

Patricio and Miguel are in the writer's study. The picture window is wide open and the silence barely perturbed by the music trickling in from the greenhouse.

Curious, Miguel crosses over to examine the books on the shelves.

"Did you write these?"

"Only a few of them."

"Has my Dad read them?"

"All of them. And your mother too. I'm referring to your real mother."

"Did she like them?"

Patricio nods.

"She was a great reader."

Her voice again: the muted voice that sometimes seemed to caress the air. Once after reading one of his books, she'd engaged in a protracted discussion with him about the importance of the word. "You're going to think what I'm saying is absurd, Patricio, but humanity without words would not be humanity." And she quoted a passage from St. John: *In the beginning was the word. And the word was God.*

She went on to develop a host of theories about how one should analyze a book. "It must be very frustrating for a writer to realize that the person passing judgment on a book is incapable of really reading it. I mean, he reads it, but he only absorbs it at an anecdotal level."

Unable to stop himself, he compares Dula's remarks to what Paula usually has to say. "If only your novels had happy endings." He remembers now how Paula behaved during the period when she believed she was entitled to "consider herself the lady of the house" and executed her domestic activities as if she were at the Verde Mar Hotel. "I've instructed Leticia to make us a nice paella" or "don't forget to take your cholesterol medicine, Patricio." She'd say it with a triumphant air, perhaps hoping that everyone would think of her as the woman the writer could not do without.

In any event, that afternoon at the Fiesta Mayor, something began to change in their behavior towards each other. It would have been impossible to pinpoint exactly what the change was. Nothing had caused a rift. There was no cause for distrust. But certain vague undercurrents had begun to arouse suspicions. The five of them were seated at a bar table overlooking the beach. And sometimes the effects of a few drinks can create miniature powder kegs capable of igniting tiny, but unfortunate crises.

They were discussing Thailand, the splendor of its scenery, its magnificent, the beauty of its women. And suddenly Rodolfo's joke: "Did you know that during the Vietnam war, Bangkok was little more than a sex spa?"

Dula appeared to be unfazed. Taking a sip from her glass, she turned towards Liaño and responded evenly, "Make sure you don't bite your tongue, Rodolfo. You might poison yourself." And with the same equanimity, she added that while Thai women might be liberal, they were also respectable.

Patricio glanced at his son. Clearly he had not appreciated Rodolfo's insinuation, yet he too remained impassive.

On the way back to Mas Delfín, Dula got into her father-in-law's car. "Find some soft music," she suggested, as he turned the radio dial. He found some oldies, from a time that no longer existed. "Don't change it," she implored him, brushing his hand. I like the old ballads."

Then he asked her whether Rodolfo's comment had bothered her. "Not at all. Frankness does not wound when it is not intended to wound. Besides," she added smiling, "Rodolfo was absolutely right. During the Vietnam war, Bangkok was a whorehouse."

*　　*　　*

Miguel has now discovered what a merry-go-round is, and bumper cars, and the Persian wheel, and all manner of new games heretofore unknown to him.

Grandfather has wanted his grandson to experience the emotions of all the different rides.

"Come on, Miguel, now we'll ride these horses."

They are made of wood. They wear fierce expressions and gaudily painted manes, but they seem real to Miguel. Especially when grandfather, with a determined air, climbs onto the horse next to him and assumes the posture of a real cowboy.

"Hold on tight to the reins and watch how I do it," he says.

The music starts and the merry-go-round begins to turn. The music is tinny and strident, piercing the air with its festive melody.

"Squeeze with your knees so you don't fall off."

And Miguel feels tall and elegant like El Cid.

But most exciting of all is his grandfather's joy.

"Come on, gallop. Like this. Pretend we're riding across an open field."

73

Miguel laughs. It is the nervous laughter of one who is living the full range of his imagination, from sadness to euphoria.

And grandfather is abetting him. He is certain Miguel will never forget what he is experiencing at this moment and so he tries to spur him to even greater delight.

"Are you having fun?"

Miguel does not respond. He just nods and smiles.

Indeed, to Miguel's way of thinking, this afternoon surpasses any other possible pastime. Although he cannot articulate it, he knows his grandfather has become much more than that to him. He's more like a buddy. A close friend able to transport him to a fantastic world of human magnetisms, dancing colors, and fascinating sounds.

"Now what?" he asks, when they descend from the merry-go-round.

There are a lot of "whats" still to be explored. They need to try the Mansion of Horrors and the Target Shoot and the Whip, and the Superman who can carry them off to his home planet.

The promised ice cream still awaits and the *churros*, those long round tubes with their tempting aroma of fried dough.

"What is the Mansion of Horrors?" inquires Miguel.

"A place that is scary but nothing bad happens."

"I want to see it."

"Are you sure?"

"Yes. If it's just pretend scary it doesn't matter."

Clearly Miguel is trying to act brave, but he can't quite suppress a slight shiver of fear of the unknown.

The Mansion of Horrors is right there, its cardboard façade painted to resemble the terrifying face of a monster, its jaws wide open.

"You have to go in through that mouth."

Miguel does not like the monster's huge maw.

"We should just forget it," grandfather recommends.

But the child is insistent.

"I want to go in."

All at once sinister music begins to play, complete with blood-curdling screams, wailing, howling and banging drums. Still, the child does not shrink back. He grabs onto his grandfather convinced that as long as he is there, nothing bad can happen to him.

They settle into a sort of train that begins to move almost immediately. And then the darkness, the macabre surprises, the catastrophic scenes: flying bats, ghosts lying in ambush, devils spewing flames from their mouths, disembodied heads talking, floating skulls in search of their skeletons, which are dancing about in confusion as they await their heads. And ghouls, lots of ghouls, with their scythes poised to chop off heads or mutilate corpses as they attempt to flee in horror.

"Don't be afraid, Miguel."

The child does not respond. He clutches his grandfather, his eyes squeezed shut.

"It's all fake," he says soothingly.

But Miguel does not want to look. Miguel knows if he looks he will not be able to be alone, or sleep, or move about the big house at Mas Delfín in peace.

"Come, hold on to me."

And the boy buries his face in his grandfather's chest, as the car in which they are riding descends rapidly towards the final experience.

Then back into the light and normalcy, the child's blond hair plastered to his forehead with sweat.

"You didn't like it, right?"

Miguel is not sure. He is dazed. The only thing he is knows for sure is that his grandfather's body has defended him once more against those internal assaults that sometimes leave him convulsed with fear.

"I prefer the merry-go-round."

"We won't go back in that place ever again, Miguel. I promise. I don't like that sort of thing either."

At that, the child stops walking. He looks up at him gratefully and asks for a piggy-back ride because he is tired.

That night, his grandfather puts him to bed. Leticia has already helped him with his prayers and Patricio stays behind to tell him a story with good guys and bad guys.

But the child is sleepy.

"Just rub my head, Grandfather."

That makes him even drowsier. His grandfather's hand stroking his neck and forehead is like a sedative.

"Good night, little fellow."

"Good night, Grandfather."

"Happy dreams."

And he gently touches his lips to the child's forehead.

"I love you, you know that, little fellow? I love you so much."

"I love you too," the child answers, his eyes closed.

"I'm going to have a hard time getting used to living without you when you leave."

"I won't leave."

His voice is almost imperceptible, as if it is not he who is speaking, but rather some far away self that refuses to accept reality.

And once again, Patricio recalls Dula's voice telling him something similar. "Living in Mas Delfín is like going back to your childhood."

That long ago afternoon she too had gone into the Mansion of Horrors, just as her son had done today, and she had ridden the wooden horses, and the Persian wheel, and the bumper cars.

He recalls her teasing. Entering the Mansion of Horrors, she had moved close to her husband and feigning fear, had begged Gregorio to defend her. "I'm scared, Gregorio. I'm really really scared." Gregorio had laughed as he hugged her close. "Don't forget, I'm just a defenseless little Thai girl who only knows about Chinese dragons." He also recalls his son's laughter, still so forthright, so serene, and confident.

After that, they had ridden the bumper cars, those out-of-control vehicles with nonfunctional steering wheels. The worst part was Paula's shrill wails when Gregorio and Dula crashed into their car.

Paula had stayed behind at the hotel that evening and Dula, perhaps to avoid Liaño, had gotten into her father-in-law's car.

Once again, her scent of violets permeated everything. And the old-time music Dula liked so much. And the silence.

He is remembering now how nightfall had crept up on them slowly. It was a clear, warm night. It was absurd to talk. Talking can be the most maladroit way of causing the parapets to come tumbling down. They had only mentioned the Liaño remark. Then the gentle music. And then the silence.

They had parted as soon as they arrived at Mas Delfín and did not meet again until dinner.

That night it was Rodolfo who dominated the conversation. The others seemed too tired to voice an opinion. Out of nowhere, Gregorio asked Liaño a question, which came out more like a threat. "Tell me, Rodolfo, are you going to remain at Mas Delfín all summer?"

Judging from the rapid-fire response, it seemed as if Rodolfo had been anticipating the question. "It is quite possible that I shall take a vacation at the end of July. You're father doesn't usually need me in August and September."

* * *

Patricio Gallardo provided all manner of entertainment for his grandson from the day he arrived at Mas Delfín. There were costumes of every sort, nighttime stories about Power Rangers or galactic heroes, and underwater discoveries. He even taught him how to interpret fish language. "Listen to that conch, Miguel. Pay close attention to what it is telling you. Fish understand the conches perfectly, so if you learn their language, you'll end up being able to communicate with all of them."

And Miguel would follow along because he knew his grandfather would never let him down. At first he had a hard time understanding what the conches were telling him, but he soon began to capture the sense of the language. "Only children are capable of learning these things," his grandfather insisted. It did not even occur to Miguel that what he was hearing was a product of his own imagination. Little fantasies to match his grandfather's.

Sometimes when they didn't have much to talk about, grandfather and grandson would sit side by side on the beach contemplating the sea, each immersed in his own internal dialogue, manufacturing dreams that probably would never come true. But it did not matter. Sometimes dreaming is a way of living things that might never become actual experiences.

What took up much of their time, however, was grandfather's plan to celebrate the boy's birthday to the nines.

"I'm going to invite a lot of children," he promised.

For this he turned to Paula for help. There were always a lot of children—tourists—willing to participate in whatever Paula suggested or planned.

And something else major was in the works too. Miguel was angling to get his grandfather to buy him a dog. Leticia was the one who'd put the idea in his head. "There used to be a dog named Brutus at Mas Delfín. . . . " And he did not let up until his grandfather agreed to take him into the city to get another Brutus.

And that's where they are going now, by car, with Liaño at the wheel. It is a happy trip and a chance for the child to learn new things. He notices every detail. "What is that post for?" or "Why does that man have a beard?" or "How come the houses aren't painted like in Thailand?"

The fields they pass seem strange to him too. He is used to vast plains and rice paddies, and herds of buffalo running amok on the farmers' lands.

This city also lacks a river. It has no canals or storefront houses lining the banks. No gondolas float peacefully along on the water to sell food to the inhabitants as they shield themselves from the scorching sun under their large, pagoda-shaped straw hats or seek the shade of palm trees, whose swaying branches offer cool respite to passersby.

"There are no rivers or floating markets here."

But he likes the city. There are things about it he does not understand, but he likes it nonetheless.

"Where are the portraits of the Monarchs?" he asks. In Bangkok the portraits are frequently visible on storefronts and walls.

"What monarchs?"

"You know, Sirikit and Bhumibol."

"They are not kings and queens of Spain."

"And what are the monarchs of Spain like?"

"Good and intelligent."

"Like those in Thailand?"

"Maybe even better."

"But Mom says the ones in Thailand are the best in the world."

The child is recalling his parents' evening conversations in Bangkok, while he played in the adjoining room. He did not understand exactly what they were saying and, consequently, the messages he had extracted were a little sketchy. The discussions actually were to the effect that the Thai people could accept their monarchs' diplomatic efforts to mediate between the military and democratic forces, as long as the country was able to shed its feudal agricultural system to become one of the economic "tigers" of Asia. Of this, Miguel understood just two things: monarchs are good, and Thailand is a tiger.

It does not take them long to get to the pet store. Most of the dogs for sale are puppies. But Miguel is having a hard time choosing. He hesitates. He glances towards his grandfather seeking advice, but he is still not sure which one to choose.

"Come on now, pick one. Which one do you like the best?"

In the end he picks a full-grown, but still young dog.

"The one with long ears."

The breed does not matter. Miguel has chosen it because he likes the way it looks. It has brown fur with lots of black spots.

Leticia likes it too.

"The last thing we need is for it to escape like the other one."

Miguel is not worried. He is convinced the new Brutus is a devoted and responsible dog. And it isn't for nothing that he's going to be the one in charge of taking care of its every need.

"Well that's it then, as long as you're going to take care of the mutt."

Sometimes Leticia is unbearable. Especially when she scolds Miguel for the "restless imagination" he inherited from God knows who.

It's all because Miguel likes to create unusual situations: games with no name that only his grandfather knows how to play with him.

Not Leticia. Leticia only knows how to play hide-and-seek and step on the plants in the garden to make Canuto mad so he'll pronounce the mysterious word that grandfather says has to do with a glass of milk. Leticia also likes to read certain magazines with photographs of people who later appear on TV.

"There must be a reason they pay so much attention to those "moms" and those newborn babies, and those dark-skinned kinky-haired people."

The fact is that Leticia has very particular preferences and does not allow anyone to argue with her about them. So when Miguel starts imagining things about the shape of a rock, the flight of a bird, or the colors of a butterfly, Leticia loses her temper and tells him straight out to stop talking nonsense and "edify" himself by examining "the saints" who bring us such enlightening magazines.

"You've got to come down out of the clouds, Miguel. Don't get stuck up there like your grandfather sometimes does. The most important thing is to always be well-informed."

Sometimes the friction between Miguel and Leticia spirals out of control and that's when she threatens him with severe punishments.

"You're not having any chocolate until you say you're sorry."

But the child will not back down.

"Well, if you don't give me any chocolate, I won't give you the photos I promised you, and besides, I'm going to put a lizard in your bed while you're sleeping."

He says it with the severe expression that calls for him to frown and cross his arms over his chest. And then Leticia gets exasperated and christens him with the hateful name of Mr. Proper.

"Look at him, doctor. If Miguel isn't Mr. Proper then you tell me who is."

During such scenes, Miguel often would run up the stairs to his room in a fury and fling himself across his bed to cry. Then Patricio would hurry after him. He'd go over to the bed, gather him up in his arms and rock him like a baby. "Come on Miguel. Leticia was just kidding. We all love you," until the child had calmed down.

But after buying the dog this afternoon, everything is smooth as silk at Mas Delfín.

All of a sudden, grandfather bursts into the kitchen to summon him.

"I want to introduce you to someone who is going to help us organize your birthday party."

And taking Miguel by the hand, he leads him into the sitting room, where Paula is waiting, tall and svelte, her body sheathed in a pair of skimpy shorts and a tight fitting t-shirt.

"I'd like you to meet Miguel," Patricio says with a formal air.

But when Paula bends down to kiss him, Miguel flinches.

"And who are you? My grandmother?"

The child's notion causes Patricio to smile and Paula to scowl.

"She could be, but she is not. Paula is the person in charge of making sure your birthday party is a success."

"Oh, okay."

"Don't worry, Miguel. I'll make sure lots of kids come and everything is perfect."

But despite Paula's good intentions and efforts to seem nice, Miguel cannot bring himself to like her.

"We'll make you a delicious cake and you can blow out the candles."

"Okay."

But he is not interested in what Paula is telling him. What does concern him is that his grandfather not get distracted by this "gigantic auntie who never stops talking."

"Do you know what, Miguel? I knew your mother years ago."

The dead lady again. The memory in the photograph again.

"My mother is in Brazil," he bristles.

And Paula realizes she's put her foot in it and, as Patricio has told her at least a thousand times, "you would have been even more beautiful if you'd just kept your mouth shut."

Undeterred, she merely keeps on prattling. To distract the boy, she starts going on about the tourists at the Verde Mar Hotel, the attire of the English, the food preferences of the Germans, the trouble the French girls get into with the waiters, the Arab sheiks always surrounded by women, and the Texas millionaires.

Paula does not understand the notion of boundaries. And when she gets all worked up, there is no stopping her.

"Enough."

It is a terse, peremptory "enough." The "enough" of someone who has put up with her ridiculous verbiage for years. Paula stops talking instantly.

"It's probably best you leave, Paula. We will discuss this further some other time," recommends Patricio.

Paula is unconcerned. She understands. She accepts. She's been with this man for too long to make the mistake of standing up to him. That is why it doesn't bother her in the least to act submissive and swallow her pride.

Paula is also aware that she has limitations, her gorgeous figure notwithstanding. For six years now, Patricio has been pounding the idea into her head so she does not make the mistake of getting too full of herself. "You're just like a fish. Your mouth is your downfall." And she's heard it so many times she has come to believe it.

She is also convinced—since Patricio has made it clear to her at least a thousand times—that she lacks the gift of tact, and balance and sense, which would make up for her lack of intelligence.

So when she goes overboard and tries to act "in the know" she finds herself walking on quicksand. Her feet go under and the more she tries to free herself, the deeper she sinks. "Try to control yourself, Paula. You always end up making a fool of yourself. And please, pay attention to your tone of voice. Try to modulate it a little. And most of all, just keep your opinions to yourself. No one cares whether you have bought a bikini, or went into the city to visit your Aunt Dominga, or that a high school friend is staying at the Verde Mar Hotel. No one is interested in hearing about how the graduating class of such and such a year gets together to celebrate the fact they are still alive."

But when she lets her guard down, Paula forgets Patricio's advice and launches right back into her prattle, punctuated with nasal snorts, and tedious explanations.

The only thing she keeps hanging on to is the impact of her figure. And the admiration she inspires in the hotel's patrons. And how romantic it was when she first met Patricio.

This does not, however, keep her from experiencing the occasional sense of nostalgia or the need to be something more than a magnificent animal. Especially when she recalls the far-off Dula's personality.

Even Paula could see that Dula, while not outwardly spectacular, seemed to possess a powerful hidden magic, which rendered her unforgettable. And then there was her voice. Her way of reasoning. And her smile. "I want to be like her," Paula told Rodolfo Liaño once. But he merely shook his head from side to side. "Impossible, Paula. Dula is one of a kind. They broke the mold."

＊　＊　＊

I remember the night we had the party at Mas Delfín to celebrate the kid's arrival. The moon was huge and white, as if it had been custom-made for the occasion. I remember the long strip formed by its reflection on the water as it traveled towards the horizon.

Everything looked different that day. Additional lighting illuminated the greenhouse and Canuto had spent all afternoon polishing the windows so the flowers could be seen from the esplanade and the terrace. "You are to be congratulated, Rodolfo. The setting is impressive," I told him. "I knew you wouldn't let me down."

The entrance soon filled with cars. Neighbors from along the coast, literary colleagues, editors, a world of important people were heading for the party that promised to be the biggest bash of the summer.

Liaño had outdone himself with the physical setting. He'd arranged for parking in the wooded area adjacent to the esplanade.

Tables had been set up on either side of the greenhouse for food and drink. Others lined the extensive terrace, covered with red tablecloths and ringed by white chairs.

But most spectacular by far was the way in which the forest had been illuminated. It was a young wood and its vivid green hues cast mysterious shadows on unfathomable depths of trees, leaves, and branches.

As I recall, Paula—who had only recently joined our family circle—got her fill of dancing with most of the men there, exuding the breezy confidence of a woman sure of her charms, while never letting me out of her sight in case I needed her. In those days, Paula still believed that what we had, no matter how trivial it might seem, could turn into love.

I can hear the sounds too: a jumble of voices, rustling silk, firm steps and gentle music. I can still distinguish the aromas of mineral salts and hot humid air, of perfume, and woods. And I see Gregorio introducing his wife as if she were a prize. "Dula, her name is Dula."

It would be two months before the couple returned to Thailand. Two months overloaded with all manner of bewildering circumstances. I could not make up my mind whether I was going to find the visit too long or too short.

At her husband's request, Dula was wearing a Thai outfit that evening. It's as if I'm seeing her move about in that graceful manner of hers, as if she were going to perform a traditional dance from her country, smiling at the guests and gazing at her husband with the accustomed poise that had so captivated him. "I'm glad people can see you dressed as you were on the day I asked you to marry me."

And I hear Liaño asking me some trivial question about the drinks or the refreshments planned for the early morning hours.

But my strongest memory is of the moment when an enthusiastic Gregorio came up to me, Dula at his side, and asked me to dance with her. "It's time you danced with my wife, Dad."

We approached the dance floor. Paula was there too, but I did not even notice her. I noticed Dula's body close to mine, her left arm pressing lightly against my right arm, as if to keep me at a slight distance. I don't know what I felt. It was like a tremor that immediately left me dazed.

Her waist was supple and every inch of her smelled of violets. There was a moment when my chin brushed her forehead. I noticed it was hot. Yet when I looked at her face, it was pallid. And all at once, the feeling of detachment, as if we were the only two people there. And a lengthy silence. We danced without words. Just music. Soft melodies because Dula had confessed to me that she liked the oldies.

The orchestra was playing "Unforgettable." For years, whenever I heard that song it reminded me of Juliana. But at that moment, Juliana became a blur. She stopped being unforgettable. Or maybe her enduring essence was transferred to the woman dancing with me. I felt as if the only prevailing truth in that moment was the music.

And then the threat of time. The immutable factor. It flows on and nothing and no one can hold it back.

Suddenly the music launched into the first strains of another song, "When I fall in love it will be forever." And Dula broke the silence by remarking that "forever" was the most elegant way to pay homage to the word "never." And as she spoke, her body stiffened and the hand on my arm turned to lead.

Until the music changed again and Dula fled without a word, leaving me standing there on the dance floor.

"Are you having fun, Miguel?"

But Miguel, his head spinning, does not hear his grandfather. The party that has been organized to celebrate his fifth birthday exceeds the child's wildest expectations. His ears hear only the hubbub and his eyes are soaking up the thousand and one surprises Rodolfo Liaño has prepared for him.

Since the children from the Verde Mar Hotel arrived, it's been nothing but boisterous activity: clowns, sack races, blindfolds, sticks for hitting the bags of candy, and sleight-of-hand tricks. Everything has been carefully anticipated so that Miguel's fifth birthday will be permanently engraved onto the esplanade like an indelible milestone.

"Get ready to blow out the candles."

And Miguel—who has quickly befriended this group of children he has never set eyes on before today—turns to his grandfather, his face glowing with excitement.

"They're going to bring a cake?" he asks, his eyes opened wide.

Mas Delfín has become a battlefield. It is a culture broth of illusions, enthusiastic voices, and nervous footsteps. And a heap of streamers, paper hats and strident noisemakers, which echo the shrieking voices, amplifying the childish delirium and filling the air with joy.

That afternoon, just as on the other occasion six years before, they have set up tables with red tablecloths and chairs near the greenhouse and thanks to Paula, the Verde Mar Hotel has taken care of all the details. Waiters serve mugs of chocolate, or trays of appetizers, pastries, sweets, and little meat pies. Babysitters had been sent to watch over the little ones and distribute goody bags and balloons and soccer jerseys. Nothing must be wanting at Miguel Gallardo's party.

The child's excitement grows as the cake arrives with its five lighted candles and the hosts begin to sing Happy Birthday. Miguel is all puffed up. He has never felt this important in his entire life. Even Leticia—who has put on her best outfit in honor of the occasion—is being nice to him.

"Come on, my boy, blow out the candles."

And Miguel puffs out his cheeks to blow them all out at once.

"That's it. Strong."

Even Brutus, who does not leave the boy's side, is riled up by all the racket.

The din must be making him nervous because all of a sudden he starts to bark. His sharp, reedy yips echo his young owner's infectious delight.

"Brutus, quiet boy."

But Brutus will not be quiet. Brutus is the official last word on every happiness, illusion, or activity that involves Miguel.

The day had started early, at the exact moment when his grandfather had come into his room with the promised gift.

"Happy birthday, Miguel."

And without giving the child a chance to even blink, he had placed the bicycle on the bed.

"Do you like it?"

Miguel could not believe it. No one had ever given him such an important present.

He reached out and hugged him.

"I love you grandfather. I love you so much."

But he did not wait for his grandfather to respond. With a single leap he was on his feet and, grasping the bike as best he could, he rushed down the steps to ride from one end of the terrace to the other.

At the accustomed swimming time, while Liaño and his "almost grandmother" Paula are setting up tables, hanging streamers, and preparing the wealth of surprises that await the child later in the afternoon, he and his grandfather had gone down to the beach to get the fishing gear. And because it was his birthday, the fishing was better than ever.

"Are you happy, Miguel?

The afternoon is over and night falls on Mas Delfín with the lethargy that follows a prolonged period of commotion.

Miguel nods in silence, but he is drowsy and his eyelids are drooping so his grandfather gathers him up and carries him to bed.

"Will you rub my head, grandfather?" he asks softly, because sleep has prevailed over speech and he can hardly get the words out.

His grandfather's hand strokes his head and neck gently, then kisses him lightly on the forehead.

"Good night, little fellow."

But the child does not answer. He is an angel in the making who has been overtaken by sleep.

His grandfather leaves the room and goes out onto the terrace.

It is not yet completely dark. The evening is clear. The twinkling stars give the impression that they are there for the sole purpose of illuminating the landscape.

But the landscape has been defiled, broken, and torn apart in all the chaos.

Nothing is in its place. It is a mishmash of overturned tables, upset chairs, napkins, party hats and streamers.

It reminds him of that other evening, after the party Patricio had thrown for the kids. The esplanade, the terrace, and the woods of Mas Delfín had looked much as they do now after Miguel's party.

Patricio had slept fitfully that night. A certain nagging of his conscience had kept him awake. He felt as if something very powerful—something he had not anticipated—was turning him into a different kind of being. Someone who, in a sense, had become a fugitive from himself, a thief of his own personality.

The worst part was his evident inability to self-analyze and organize his thought processes. In fact, he tried not to think because to do so was to lose impetus and bury illusions. Especially if—as it was beginning to dawn on him—the fear lying in wait for him got a hold of his mind.

It was morning before he fell asleep.

Rain was pouring down and from the balcony the garden looked a little hung over. It was an ill-tempered morning, resembling the end of the day more than the beginning.

Tossed napkins, dumped ashtrays, shards of shattered glasses scattered over the lawn, articles left behind by a distracted guest, and the whole mess battered by the rain. Footprints and mud had turned Mas Delfín's usually bucolic, peaceful aspect into an etching cut with crude, detached strokes.

Not much light. Lots of dark patches. Even the sea looked different. Overnight it had turned hostile, headstrong, and frothy. Breakfast was meager; no one else was in the dining room.

But when he returned to his study, Liaño was there on the balcony. "Your editor called me yesterday evening to say the novel is taking too long," he said pointblank. His editor was right. He had not spent a single day writing since the kids had arrived. "What are you insinuating? That I'm not a professional?" he answered in a joking tone, brushing aside the whole matter. Indeed, the beginning of the novel was there, ensconced in a plastic case like someone in a coma waiting to return to consciousness. "The truth is, Rodolfo, I can't seem to write right now. Ever since Dula and Gregorio arrived I feel as if time is standing still."

He recalls Liaño's curt and vaguely threatening response. "The trouble is that time never stands still." Patricio had failed to grasp what Liaño was trying to convey. "Explain what you mean." But Liaño persisted, "What is more, time devours, it murders, especially its own children. Remember the legend of Chronos? And seeing that Patricio did not react. "Remember what I'm going to tell you. Be careful with the thrills of the present. It may be they are too ephemeral to be taken seriously."

And it dawned on Patricio that Liaño had understood the previous evening better than he himself had. "Think it over carefully, Patricio. Don't let the present destroy your future." And after a moment's hesitation, "Fight against Chronos. Don't let him devour you. And remember that time only preserves what never comes to pass."

✳   ✳   ✳

By the time August arrived, however, a lot of things had come to pass. Frictions that were barely noticeable yet caused certain misgivings and stabs of distrust. Trifling things that could easily lead to laughter or else prompt some sign of ill-humor.

There were a few tense moments brought on for unexpected reasons. For example, Paula's tone of voice when, following an exchange with Dula, she'd come to me looking offended. "That daughter-in-law of yours likes to humiliate me."

In vain I tried to investigate what exactly this humiliation entailed. Paula could not explain it. "All I know is, she humiliates me."

She did not realize that her humiliation stemmed from an inferiority complex whenever Gregorio's wife expounded on some subject about which she knew nothing. "There is no understanding her. She absolutely infuriates me sometimes."

But what really infuriated Paula was Dula's self-confidence, her simplicity, and her way of attracting attention without meaning to and without resorting to the wiles that saved Paula from insignificance.

Still, Paula was not the only one who began to obsess about Dula. Gregorio also had begun to show signs of antagonism. He could not countenance the fact that Rodolfo had become so friendly with his wife. There was no way Gregorio could have known that the friendship essentially was my daughter-in-law's refuge from me. "Certain things about the man make me sick. Don't ask me why, Dad, but I sometimes find the way he operates repulsive."

Other sorts of tensions further charged the atmosphere but were harder to pin down. Certain looks or excuses for instance. Subtle pretexts which could somehow distort the reality of the situation.

"You're mistaken, Gregorio. I've known Rodolfo for years. It's not what you imagine."

But my explanations only served to tighten the Gordian knot that was forming. "Say what you will, Dad, Liaño really has an effect on Dula. My wife hasn't been the same person since we arrived at Mas Delfín."

Gregorio was right. Dula's personality had been changing gradually. She was becoming introverted and whenever she participated in one of our activities she appeared distracted, as if her mind was elsewhere.

By then, Dula and I no longer allowed ourselves to be alone together. We had put a stop to the visits to the greenhouse, the boat trips, and anything else that might facilitate our communication.

It was clear we had both realized the risk inherent to deepening our friendship, as she apparently was doing with Liaño. He was indeed her refuge, her strategy to keep away from me.

But there was no way for Gregorio to know that. "I'd like to know what the hell he talks to Dula about that she finds so fascinating."

I don't remember exactly when my daughter-in-law and I started to keep our distance from each other, but I have in my mind a beginning, a completely unexpected occurrence that somehow altered our easy rapport and established once and for all a new pattern of behavior between us.

It happened on a windy morning. Rebellious, angry crosswinds were blowing every which way, so that it seemed as if each discreet patch of water was trying to liberate itself from the others, feigning small schismatic spurts with no attempt at synchronization. Each one seemed to be facing off with another, surging into crests of disjointed waves, hysterical and violent. "It's like a sea on the verge of declaring war," exclaimed Rodolfo.

And when Dula asked in a joking voice who the enemy was, Liaño turned towards her and echoing her ironic tone, declared solemnly, "the sea itself. It is the law of life, Dula. We humans are also our own enemies."

That morning, Liaño decided to take the boat up the coast as if to defy the violence of the aquatic "outburst." Canuto and I warned him, to no avail, of the danger of tangling with the sea when it was covered in whitecaps and spewing foam.

It's as if I am seeing Canuto sniffing the air and looking displeased. "Do not tempt fate, Mr. Liaño. When the sea is like this it's worse than a northerly."

But Rodolfo was insistent. "I'll be back in time for lunch." And with one leap he was in the boat lunging against its tethers at the dock.

Propelled by the same sense of exhilaration, Dula grabbed her towel and, without warning, ran for the boat just as Rodolfo was starting the motor. "Wait, Rodolfo, I'll go with you."

Dula's impulsive action went unnoticed. No one was in a position to keep her from running into the sea, waving the towel so it wouldn't get wet as she approached the pitching boat.

But I saw her. And I also saw Liaño who, despite his proximity, could not hear her over the roar of the crosswinds.

It was useless to yell. No one would have been able to hear me either, much less Dula, who had just reached the prow of the vessel.

The sound of the running motor and the vehemence of the wind drowned our voices. There was no way to reach her in time. Without warning, the tossing boat stabilized into a projectile and Dula's body had no time to ward off the blow as it came down on top of her.

It was a dull thud that left her unconscious and she sunk into the water, the towel floating about her body.

At once, everything was sorrow, anguish, fear, and rage. But I reacted quickly. I jumped into the water to save her. I carried her to the beach, half-drowned, her forehead bleeding.

I remember laying her down on the beach while a terrified Gregorio tried to revive her by rubbing her hands.

"Please, Dad. Do mouth-to-mouth. I can't do it."

I did it. Her lips were cold, her skin pale, and her expression lost. I have no idea how long we were there, my son and I, trying to bring her back. The only thing I recall about those moments was Rodolfo's voice lamenting what had occurred. "My God, I didn't know she was there."

And I also remember Gregorio confronting him. "Your problem, Rodolfo, is that you don't know a lot of things."

When Dula began to come to, I picked her up and carried her to the house. Here body was as light and elastic as a young girl's. "Don't worry, Dula. You were lucky. It could have been a lot worse."

She did not speak or moan. She just stared at me. It was a beseeching look, as if she were begging me to get away from her.

We put her in bed and as soon as she was lying down, I left the room so she could be alone with my son.

It was a combative afternoon. Gregorio obstinately continued to blame Liaño for what had happened. To no avail I tried to make him see he was mistaken. "I don't see how you can be so obtuse, Gregorio. Rodolfo never suggested that Dula get into the boat." But the more I tried to calm him down, the more irritated he became. "I don't like Liaño, Dad. I can't get a handle on him. I think he's capable of doing just about anything to get what he wants."

Of everything that happened, what I recall most vividly now is Dula's expression as she lay in bed with her forehead bandaged and fear in her eyes, and begged her husband not to leave her alone.

Indeed, that day marked the beginning of the real changes. Something like the first link which, before long, would unleash the chain of excesses that followed.

The outing to the hermitage of the "saint with no name" came shortly after that.

I think I will never forget that outing. Besides, there is the walking stick Dula had given me the night before. It is a rough stick, a goatherd's staff, its curved handle slightly scorched. "I bought these walking sticks in town. Everyone says you need help if you're going to climb Daní mountain. Apparently, the path is very steep and rutted."

It is hard to explain how something as ordinary as a walking stick can evoke such inconsequential moments from the past, which are recast by time as indelible memories. But now, as I regard the staff propped here in my study, I recall every detail of the giving.

We were on the terrace and—for some unfathomable reason I no longer remember—we were alone.

I'm not sure how many days we had spent avoiding each other, but I do know we were both trying to act as if it were a perfectly normal encounter.

"It will probably take us two hours to reach the top."

"I would think so. Liaño has already bought the packs to carry our lunch."

"He says we don't have to worry about water. Apparently there's a freshwater spring near the hermitage."

"Well, thank you for the staff, Dula. It was a good idea."

We were up early the following morning. I still remember the smell emanating from the kitchen as Leticia fried potato pancakes. And Canuto's voice assuring us that the tomatoes for the salad had been picked that very morning and the fruit was so ripe that if we didn't eat it right away it would have to be thrown out.

I remember the morning sun was somewhat tempered by the mist, yet the air was clear enough that the view from the mountain top would not be obscured.

The path was steep and by the time we'd reached the halfway mark the four of us—Paula was working and had been unable to join us—were out of breath. We stopped to rest.

Suddenly, and for no reason, the four of us burst out laughing. I suppose the altitude was starting to make us a little giddy. Even Dula seemed to recover the vivacity she'd exhibited when she first arrived from Thailand.

"The three of you have definitely gone soft," she said, pointing to the goatherd's staffs. "Come on now, three big strong men."

And she continued up the path, encouraging us to follow. I remember we occasionally looked back to see how far we had come. As we climbed, the town seemed to shrink, while the sea expanded.

"Come on, no resting. We need to get to the hermitage soon."

Dula again, perched on a knoll. From below, her body seemed elongated and as she sliced the air with the staff, she resembled a cornstalk swaying in the wind.

The terrain was rough and precipitous and the path was hard to discern. Time and vegetation had erased it. Because of this, the hermitage—once the site of pilgrimages, promises, and testimonies of faith—was falling to ruin.

Nowadays no one bothered to climb the mountain to ask the saint to perform a miracle. The lethargy of the apathetic and the cynicism of self-styled sophisticates had gradually eroded the meaning of its existence.

All that remained was the historic structure, albeit in a state of total disrepair for lack of maintenance.

I still recall Rodolfo's jokes: "Coming here isn't about visiting the saint anymore. It's to give yourself a killer workout."

But Dula was not ready to let go of the traditional aspect.

"I have been told this saint really does perform miracles." What bothered her was not knowing his name. If only she knew what it was.

I explained to her once more that the hermitage had always belonged to the fishermen. And the fact was, the townspeople had no real desire to know the saint's name.

But Dula seemed not to hear. Something was on her mind and she was not in the mood for any intrusions.

That day turned out to be crucial to what came later. But at the time we had no way of knowing what was going to happen.

There is the smell of charred firewood coming from an improvised cook fire where Dula roasted lamb chops. And Rodolfo's voice announcing that it was raining on the far side of Mas Delfín.

After lunch, Gregorio and Rodolfo began to doze off. I too pretended to be asleep, but it was a pretext to avoid having to talk to her. Then I saw Dula walk over to the hermitage.

The gate was locked, yet she pushed on it as if she might be able to open it. It held fast. What came next was astonishing. She fell to her knees before the gate and began to sob.

4

When Miguel is in a bad mood for some reason, he starts in with Leticia.

"I don't like this food."

"Well, it's all I have."

"I don't care. I just won't eat then."

"You little devil. How do you know you don't like it when you haven't even tasted it?"

But Miguel is not interested in logic. Miguel has gotten up on the wrong side of the bed this morning. And no matter how hard she tries, Leticia is getting nowhere with him.

It is all because his grandfather has gone to the city without him. It did not matter that he had tried to prepare him. "I have to go to the city to settle a matter with my editor." The reasons make no difference to him. What hurts is that grandfather has not included him in this trip. But he doesn't say that. He just acts it out. And Leticia is quite incapable of keeping him from getting so worked up.

"One of these days, I'm going to leave here and you'll never see me again."

"Yes. And then you'll have to figure out what to do when it comes time to answer to God."

But Miguel is furious and as he vents his eyes fill with tears and his voice breaks until it is nothing more than a weak thread.

"So here we have Mr. Proper again."

Right then, Leticia is nothing but a hateful old fatso who jiggles when she walks and gets so overheated from carrying around all that weight that her underarms become stained with sweat and her hair sticks to her chest.

"And you're the old witch with the candy house."

Leticia is unmoved. Leticia has the virtue of being able to wrap herself in an invisible cloak that shields her from any verbal onslaught. Instead, she brings up tidbits from the past to humiliate the boy.

"You know what, Mr. Proper? When your father was your age, he was not all cross like you are. He was the nicest boy in the world. You should follow his example."

But Miguel does not reply. Still offended, he jumps from his chair and leaves the house.

It has been a boring morning. There was no swim, no grandfather's voice telling him stories about the fish and the birds and everything, which Miguel listens to with rapt attention. Especially when they hike in the woods and he ignites the boy's curiosity by telling him how the trolls and gnomes who live there hide behind the oak trees when they sense the approach of a human.

And the sky is overcast to boot. The day is like lead and the clouds obscure the hermitage at the top of Daní mountain.

One might say it is a lifeless day. It is impossible to find anything to shake him out of this bad mood. Instead of lifting his spirits, every single thing seems to be against him. Even the bicycle. There it is, discarded and scorned as if it had never been the child's dream at all. And Brutus, wagging his tail and sniffing around his sneakers to get him to play, is ignored too, because not even the dog interests him today.

Miguel is bored. He is bored just like caged birds, or moles, or bats are.

Then he spies the soccer ball, resting against a pot of geraniums. And he recalls with nostalgia how his grandfather taught him to shoot and steal the ball from the other team. Grandfather knew everything and talked to him about everything—and showed him fascinating things when they'd sit down to watch TV.

Because now Miguel even knows who Beckham is and the importance of soccer. And he can't even think about going down to the beach without being able to make goals with grandfather and feel a little bit like Beckham.

Then he spies Canuto. He has not gone down to the beach today either. Right now he is crossing the wooded area with a look of fatigue, heading towards the foot of the bluff and the greenhouse. Canuto has his routines and he never forgets to take care of the flowers and plants in that place, even though grandfather never shows much interest in those flowers. Miguel has not forgotten a conversation between Patricio and the groundskeeper a few days ago. "Don't you think after all this time it might not make sense to just raze the greenhouse and let everything in it die once and for all?"

Canuto is slightly deaf but Miguel is convinced he was only pretending not to hear what grandfather was saying. "Did you say something about flowers?" And grandfather, "Indeed I did, Canuto. Who really cares if they stay alive?" And while he might be a rough-hewn man, Canuto always has a ready answer to uphold his principles. "Miss Paula likes to decorate the house with flowers."

But grandfather is having none of it. "Miss Paula is not one to decide what goes on at Mas Delfín." And seeing that Canuto had just stood there open-mouthed, "I'm not asking you to destroy them, Canuto. I'd just like you to let them die. Put an end to the comedy once and for all, putting on music to sooth them and all that ridiculous talking to them. In short, just forget about them."

But Canuto cannot forget about them. He has spent too many years assimilating Mrs. Juliana's beliefs to suddenly turn his back on them. Canuto is a creature of habit and those habits are his credo. So every day, when he has a free moment, he goes to the greenhouse to take care of the plants.

But Miguel has never gone in there. Every time he asks his grandfather to show it to him, he gets evasive and changes the subject. Which is why he feels now might be a good time to go in there and see the place.

Canuto is not a dimwit like Leticia, nor does he call him "Mr. Proper" or throw in his face that his father was the most perfect boy in the world when he was little. Canuto is simply an expert on the sea, and flowers, and climbing, and the sky, and butterflies. And he talks to Miguel like a trusted guide, teaching the boy to identify different kinds of insects, plants, winds, clouds, and fish, without getting into off-putting dialectics.

"Wait, Canuto, I'm coming with you," yells Miguel before Canuto disappears into the greenhouse.

And without further thought, he runs towards the bluff, Brutus at his heels.

Once again, the dog's antics and barking. Canuto smiles when he sees them coming. He knows his teeth are stained from smoking so many home-made cigars, but he is not ashamed to display them. Besides, Canuto adores children and has no problem explaining down to the last detail how to find water underground with a divining rod or how to make a flat rock skip along the water by tossing it just the right way.

Canuto is clearly a man of substance whose only defect is that he does not bathe very often. Which is probably why, as he approaches Miguel, the boy senses an avalanche of disagreeable odors bearing down on him. A mixture of fodder, excavated earth, and a large helping of manure.

"Okay, go on in."

And Miguel obeys, although he is upset that Canuto will not let Brutus follow.

"It's the lady's orders, may she rest in peace. Dogs are not allowed in to the greenhouse."

"What lady?"

"Who else? Your grandmother."

"You mean Paula?"

"The devil take Paula. That young miss is not your grandmother. Wonder when you'll get it into your head. You're grandmother is in heaven."

"Well, if she doesn't know and she can't see us, what's the problem if Brutus comes in with us?"

"You have to respect the wishes of the dead."

And with that, he closed the door on the dog. Brutus scratched the door and howled in vain.

"He needs to get used to waiting for you outside like the other Brutus did."

And taking the child by the hand, he guided him along the uneven passageways of the hothouse.

Everything is new to him in this place. It doesn't even sound the same. Here the croaking of the frogs and the crickets' chirping sound different, especially when, after the song on the record player is over, the silence gives way to the voices of living creatures.

"Be very careful, Miguel. Don't touch any of the flowers," warns Canuto. "Walk around as you wish, but don't disturb them."

"Don't worry. I won't touch them."

Canuto relaxes and allows Miguel to roam about freely and discover for himself the grandeur and dominion of the plants. Once in a while he glances back towards the groundskeeper to ask what they are called. They all have names. They all have their unique identity: gladiolas, dahlias, hanging carnations, chrysanthemums, roses, petunias, nasturtiums, verbena. But Miguel doesn't care so much about the names. What fascinates him is the pattern formed by those vegetable alleyways and the way they occupy different plots of earth so that the flowers all have their own neighborhoods and homes.

"Here are the orchids," says Canuto. "They are the queens of all the flowers."

The child comes upon the furniture which Juliana had installed to make the greenhouse seem more like a sitting room. There is a sofa, loveseat, tables, lamps and something akin to a bookshelf.

"A long time ago, when your grandmother was alive, she and your grandfather would sit here for hours. They said it was the nicest room in the house."

Miguel regards it with fascination. He even feels as if he might like to know this grandmother that Canuto has described. But he cannot even imagine her.

The myths of the past can never be totally understood by the inhabitants of the present. And Miguel, though he doesn't realize it, is also a myth. A person who sometimes believes he is an astronaut, or a being from outer space, or a soccer star, or Lance Armstrong, or a mermaid catcher.

"Your grandmother always said that flowers have souls."

"And do you believe they do?"

"If so, they would have to be pretty limited."

Miguel does not understand what he means by limitations on souls. In fact, Miguel does not understand a lot of things yet, especially when he is obsessed by some notion, or else bored as he was this afternoon.

The one thing he is proud of is his threat to Leticia when he was refusing to eat. "One of these days I'm going to leave here and you'll never see me again."

And in a flash, the idea.

A brilliant idea, huge, full of expectations and emotions. An idea that will solve all of his problems and frustrations. His rage at feeling shunted aside, the shame of having been attacked by Leticia, the revenge that will wound his grandfather. It is a perfect idea and it vanquishes the boredom he's been experiencing since morning.

For the first time all day, Miguel seems animated, excited—a person in his own right, with his own personal expectations—because he is going to be vindicated at last.

It occurred to him all of a sudden, when he realized that Canuto had forgotten all about him and was busily pruning, gathering, weeding, watering, and playing the record player.

" 'Bye, Canuto."

"Goodbye Miguel. Go on back to the house and try not to upset Leticia."

But Miguel does not leave. He has found the perfect hiding place where no one will ever find him. Now they'll realize what good is, he tells himself and, without thinking twice, he goes to the center of the greenhouse and crawls under the sofa.

Then he giggles. It is a nervous giggle, as if an elf were making him do it. His heart, though, is beating hard. And his breathing comes out all ragged. But he controls himself.

He is a little uncomfortable, but it doesn't matter. Being shunted aside, abandoned, and manipulated isn't comfortable either. Besides, what Miguel wants is for the grown-ups to get scared and realize how badly they have behaved, because a child does not deserve to be left alone all day at the mercy of his boredom, or have his powerlessness exploited, or be callously abandoned to his suffering.

He is convinced that grown-ups have a lot to learn and no one teaches them because they are grown-ups. Which is why he, a child, is willing to inflict this punishment that all of the inhabitants of Mas Delfín deserve.

The important thing is to remain absolutely silent and not make any noise until Canuto leaves the building. Then the fun will begin for sure. The hard part is, Miguel has been hiding under the sofa for quite a while now and Canuto has shown no signs of leaving.

Suddenly the lights go out and Canuto opens the door. Then he hears him address Brutus.

"What the devil are you doing here, you damned dog?"

Of course, Brutus cannot reply. He just howls excitedly and seems to be pushing against Canuto, who will not let him in. Maybe he is trying to explain in his own way that his owner is still inside and if Canuto closes the door he will be left all alone in there.

But Canuto, a cultivated man, does not speak dog language and the only thing that occurs to him is to sweep up the animal in his arms and shut the greenhouse door behind him. Then the groundskeeper's footsteps can be heard, along with the dog's whining, both growing fainter by the second as he heads for the house.

Finally Miguel feels safe. His revenge is about to begin.

Tired of the position he has been in up to now, he crawls out of his hiding place and bounces on the sofa. The sofa is comfortable and soft, and big enough to seat three adults. From the armrest where he lays his head, he can contemplate the most beautiful starry view in the world. Miguel did not know that glass ceilings could reflect astral panoramas as fascinating as the one he is gazing at now.

Little by little the peaceful atmosphere calms him and he is no longer breathless as he was underneath the sofa.

The important thing now is to contemplate this infinite world of faraway lights, of illuminated pathways that traverse space and leave him nearly hypnotized. With a little imagination, Miguel could even fly up into the vast panorama of stars and feel himself inducted into worlds unknown to humankind.

He feels serene and relaxed, along with the marvelous sensation of having avenged himself. That's the main thing. The scare he's about to give Leticia, Rodolfo, and Grandfather.

He yawns. Then he curls up on his side and falls asleep.

✻   ✻   ✻

Leticia is the first to discover he is missing.

"But I saw him go into the greenhouse with Canuto," she says.

But Canuto swears up and down that the child left the greenhouse early on.

"Before the sun went down. He told me he was coming back to the house."

Rosario, the maid, affirms once again that the child has not returned.

"Dear God, what is his grandfather going to think when he returns?"

"We have to look everywhere. Maybe we should alert the Civil Guard."

Fortunately, the night is clear. The north wind has dispersed the low clouds that had presided over the earlier part of the day.

But the search is becoming increasingly arduous and futile. To no avail they have shouted his name at the echoing mountains and into the woods. Miguel does not answer and fear begins to take hold of their imaginations, sowing horrible suspicions of some irreparable harm.

"My God, I don't even want to think what might have happened to him."

Everyone's nerves are on edge. It is the niggling fear produced by a guilty conscience. The thought that the blame for the disappearance lies not with the child, but with all of those who failed to look after him.

"God only knows what has become of him," insists Leticia. "Just this afternoon he told me he was going to leave the house and never come back."

She has confessed this in a voice choked with anguish and her eyes are reddened by unshed tears.

It does not help that Canuto and Rosario are convinced he could not have left the farm. It is a large estate and Leticia is very superstitious and always inclined to imagine the worst.

"He could have fallen."

The notion that Miguel could have plunged into a gully or fallen off the steep bluff with no one there to aid him is the worst of the scenarios that have gripped her imagination.

But Canuto calms her down. Canuto is an excellent climber and he is willing to take a flashlight and search every gully and crevasse on Mas Delfín.

All at once, they hear the sound of an engine and glimpse headlights as the road that wends its way down to the house is illuminated by Doctor Gallardo's approaching car. And compounding their sadness now is the horror of having to tell the grandfather about the child's abrupt disappearance.

"I'm going over to the bluff next to the greenhouse," exclaims Canuto without waiting for the vehicle to come to a halt on the esplanade.

But Leticia remains standing there with Rosario, her legs shaking, tears shimmering on her white face, and her stomach churning and gnawing at her like a wild animal.

"Blessed God, how am I going to tell him?"

No explanations are necessary. Patricio has seen immediately that something serious is going on. It is not normal that Miguel has not run out to greet him, or to see the two women standing there in the doorway, stationary, not speaking or reacting at all except for their loud, quaking sobs.

"What the hell is going on here?"

They finally explain. They tell it in fits and starts, repeating the same thing over and over again and contradicting themselves. They are trying to be precise, but end up talking in circles and making no sense whatsoever.

Liaño tries unsuccessfully to calm them down.

"Please, one at a time."

But they do not stop. They do not even hear him. All they can do is repeat over and over again that Miguel has vanished. He was in the greenhouse and then he was gone.

"But where?"

"We don't know. He's just gone. He said he was never coming back. He was very angry."

Patricio cannot take it any more. He shakes Leticia's shoulders and insists that she be more explicit.

"Is it possible to know what you mean by all this about his never coming back?"

"He was mad, Doctor. He left. Just like that."

Fortunately, Doctor Gallardo is a level-headed man and he is unmoved by Leticia's nonsense. Besides, he knows Miguel. Knows that no matter how much he might threaten, he is way too bright to actually follow through with his threats.

"Let's see. Let's go over everything that happened this afternoon."

The story gets longer and longer, spilling out all over the place before settling into a heap of contradictions. And Patricio is become increasingly impatient. The worst part is not being able to think, what with Leticia's wailing and blaming herself incessantly for not having looked after the boy properly.

"You'll have to kill me, Doctor. I can never repair the harm I've caused the poor creature."

The tension builds and Patricio can tell he is losing his temper.

Suddenly Brutus is there. He has rushed towards them barking and wagging his tail, but instead of pausing, he continues on to the greenhouse as if someone or something were in hot pursuit.

"Where has that animal come from?"

"He must have gotten out, Doctor. I shut him in the kitchen because he wanted to run off. I don't know what is going on, but the dog and the boy have been acting strangely."

Patricio and Rodolfo exchange a glance as the same idea occurs to them both at once.

"Let's follow Brutus."

Sometimes intuition does not err. It is a mathematical spurt that leaves no room for ambiguity. A tiny mental explosion that serves as an alert.

Indeed, the dog has stopped before the door of the greenhouse. But he does not calm down. He scratches the door with his nails, whines and barks, rising up with his front paws on the wood.

"Open that door right now."

The door is opened, the lights are turned on and the animal rushes frantically towards the center of the building.

And there is Miguel. Sleeping so soundly he is not even aware that they are all gazing down on his body curled up on the sofa, or that Leticia, clutching Rosario, has started to bawl hysterically because her nerves are shot.

The only one who is not satisfied with the situation is Brutus. Finding himself unrestrained, he leaps impetuously onto the child's body, licking him and whining all the while.

Miguel wakes up. It is an unusual and disconcerting awakening. Nothing around him makes any sense. Not his grandfather's amused expression, Leticia's sobs, or Brutus' excitement, and certainly not the dizzying array of flowers and plants that surrounds him.

"You've had us all worried," Liaño tells him.

And suddenly Miguel remembers. It is an unpleasant memory, and though he cannot recall exactly why, it is turning him into a bad boy. One of those twisted kids in the stories grandfather tells him before bed.

They have probably all discovered his disappearance was not an accident, was the result of a premeditated plan for revenge ever since his grandfather left him to his own devices in order to escape to the city.

"You hid, right?"

But Miguel does not reply. Right now Miguel is a criminal who has been caught red-handed and is vacillating between truth and falsehood. A defenseless being who has misbehaved and does not know how to extricate from the jam his pigheadedness has gotten him in to.

"If it weren't for Brutus, no one would have ever found you. You would have stayed in here forever."

But Miguel reacts to that right away.

"That's not true. Canuto would have found me."

"And what if Canuto, who is searching the bluff for you right now, should fall? Then no one would have come into the greenhouse and you wouldn't have been able to let anyone know you were in here."

Miguel reflects in silence and decides that his grandfather's displeasure is too mild for him to defend himself with his usual angry outbursts.

"Moreover, do you think it is nice that Leticia is so upset because of you?"

He does not say it angrily. To the contrary, he says it with a serene, almost kind expression. Maybe that is why Miguel seems increasingly miserable and anxious.

"No, Miguel. What you have done is not good at all. I want you to understand that."

And not only does Miguel understand, his grandfather's gentleness suffuses him with shame and regret.

"I never would have expected such a thing from you."

And that is the worst part for the child: his grandfather's disappointment, his grandfather's pain, his grandfather's disillusionment. But he resists saying he is sorry. To say you are sorry means to shrivel up, to be crushed into a miserable crumb worthy only of contempt.

This is actually what is causing the child so much anxiety: the contempt each person standing there surely feels towards him. The problem is solved in part when grandfather asks the others to leave him alone with the boy.

Only Brutus stays with them. Now he is a calm dog, resting quietly in his owner's lap.

"Look at me, Miguel."

And Miguel turns his gaze to meet his grandfather's, his eyes wide and his head bowed.

"Why did you do it?"

Miguel would like to explain but a certain quiver in his chin keeps him from opening his mouth and his voice seems to be stuck between those strange knots that squeeze your throat when you feel like crying.

"Come on, little fellow. It's over now."

And before the child bursts into tears, his grandfather takes him in his arms and holds him tightly against his chest. Together again, hearts beating in unison, their universe whole again.

"You don't love me any more, do you, Grandfather?" asks the child, with his lips pressed against his ear.

And Patricio kisses him in response.

"Why do you say that? How could I ever not love you? I think I loved you even before you were born."

It does not matter that the child can't possibly understand what he is trying to say. It is enough that he grasps his meaning. And the meaning is being absorbed into him like the best present in the world.

"Did you really love me before I was born?"

Doctor Gallardo nods. He has never forgotten his excitement when, two months after leaving Mas Delfín to return to Bangkok, Gregorio and Dula called him to say he was finally going to be a grandfather. "Brace yourself, Dad, because what I'm about to tell you is going to make you very happy."

The summer was over and the autumn chill had settled into the thick walls of the house at Mas Delfín. He was in his study at the time and as he spoke with Gregorio, he regarded the unfinished novel stuck in the plastic case.

"Are you there, Dad?"

"I'm here, Son. Tell me what is going on."

You're going to be a grandfather. Dula is pregnant. Did you hear me, Dad? Dula and I are going to have a baby."

He was having a hard time taking it in. But Gregorio went on, "Our dream has finally come true."

"I'm so happy for you, Son. Congratulations to you both."

"I really do feel like I'm dreaming, Dad. Dula and I were convinced it was never going to happen."

Then he asked to speak with his daughter-in-law.

"I would like to congratulate her."

She couldn't have been far, because her voice came over the telephone right away.

"Here I am. Thank you, Patricio."

Impossible to mistake her. It was the same voice that had warmed the evenings on the terrace, and the mornings on the beach, and the hike up Daní mountain.

"I wish you all the best, Dula."

And once more, "Thank you, Patricio."

Then there was a silence full of disjointed, somewhat bemused thoughts. The truth was, he had no words to express what he was feeling. Only platitudes came to mind.

"I'm delighted to know you are so happy."

And there was Gregorio's voice again.

"Can you come to Thailand when the baby is born?"

He'd said he would make every effort to visit, adding,

"It's still a long way off. What is the due date?"

Gregorio had already done the math.

"The first week of June."

Right at that moment, Doctor Gallardo seems far away. Suddenly everything has gone blank, except for his conversation with the kids before Miguel was born.

"Yes, Miguel," he tells him, "I loved you very much even before you were born."

And as Patricio speaks, the child presses against him and places a kiss on his cheek.

Then he scoops the child up in his arms and carries him to the house, while Brutus, tail high in the air and barking all the while, zigzags around them like a mad dog.

❋   ❋   ❋

It was the end of July when the tensions which already had provoked minor eruptions triggered an unpleasant explosion and irrevocably altered the normal course of the summer.

It all started when Gregorio discovered that Dula had been crying on the mountaintop while he slept.

He tried in vain to find out what had caused the unexpected tears. Dula could not explain it. She said she felt anxious, chalked it up to a stupid, hysterical outburst. And as she spoke, she looked at Rodolfo Liaño as if imploring him to save her.

The descent to Mas Delfín proceeded in silence. No matter how much Dula tried to excuse herself for having given in to an absurd melancholy, the uneasiness put a damper on the atmosphere.

I remember my son's irritation each time his wife drew near to Rodolfo Liaño. "Who knows what that son-of-a-bitch is up to." It was futile to explain that his suspicions were off base and there was nothing more than friendship between Liaño and Dula. "Can't you see how he looks at her? I've been saying this for a while now, Dad. I don't like the guy."

It was difficult to persuade my son, but even more difficult to be hovering on the margins of a bizarre vicious circle in which no one trusted anyone else and each harbored secrets we dared not reveal.

Indeed, the initial spontaneity had turned volatile. And no matter how much we tried to pretend that everything was going along as usual, nothing was the same.

The worst part was seeing the changes in Dula. Gone was the enlightened guest who had brought her sharp wit and intelligent nuances to our conversations. Her silences were increasingly prolonged and if you asked her a question, she would simply agree, as if she was having trouble understanding the question.

Her indifference to everything around her was becoming increasingly evident and if there was a difference of opinion, she did not even bother to argue. Instead, she would merely acquiesce. She would give in just like that. She had no desire to defend her ideas as before. And maybe that is why at the earliest possible opportunity, she would invent any excuse to shut herself in her room.

It was her behavior that led my son to confide his fears to me. "Dula has changed, Dad. I guess you've already realized that. But I just can't figure out what's wrong."

I remember we were on the beach at the time. Canuto was pushing the boat containing Dula and Rodolfo out to sea, as he did every day. "Sometimes we think we see a ghost simply because we are afraid they are out there, Gregorio. Most likely it is your own vulnerability that's betraying you."

The same afternoon we had to go to town to pick up my car, which was at the garage. We traveled in silence.

We stopped to collect Paula at the Verde Mar Hotel. She approached us with the same breezy confidence as always, asserting her role as the indispensable girlfriend. "I've made a dinner reservation for us in the beachfront dining room."

As usual, Paula chattered on without saying much. And as usual, she marred the atmosphere with her ineffable lack of discretion. "It's hard to believe that after four years together you two still don't have any children. Patricio would just love to be a grandfather." And turning to me, "wouldn't you, Patricio?"

Paula's comment might have appeared normal on the surface. But anyone with a little awareness could see she was rubbing salt in the wound. No one knew better than I how Dula anguished over her infertility.

Of course the table Paula had reserved at the Verde Mar Hotel that evening remained empty.

Nobody displayed any interest in staying in town after we had retrieved the car. We were all in a hurry to get back home. "We're sorry Paula, but we really cannot stay this evening."

That same afternoon, Dula vanished. "We can meet in the square," she said and disappeared down the street leaving the three of us on our own. And then Gregorio came over to me and implored me to wait for Dula. "I don't want her in the car with Liaño. Anyway, I need to speak with him."

I should have realized that something was going to happen between the two men, which would be difficult to repair afterward.

In reality, everything was difficult. To give the right answer or advice, to discern the parameters of what could be considered proper, to offer suitable reasons while avoiding any inadvertent blunder, and above all, to put an end to the enormous lie our truth was engendering.

"Be careful, Son. Don't forget that appearances can be deceiving."

I remember watching them walk off together as I waited for Dula in the fountain square.

Nothing in the town seemed as before. It was as if the fountain no longer produced its music, the streets no longer recalled their medieval pasts, and the beaches no longer parodied mythological fragments of Homeric tales. I don't know why, but in the blazing afternoon sunlight, the town seemed to me like a huge ship adrift in a thick fog, vainly seeking its course.

I waited quite a while for Dula, but there was no sign of her. Finally someone told me they had seen her go into the church. I set out to find her there. The nave was nearly empty and in shadows, and the alter-piece looked opaque, almost divested of its Christian meaning.

I quickly found her. She was on her knees next to a confessional where a priest was reading the breviary, a small lamp shedding a tenuous light on the page. She was obviously praying, her eyes closed and her hands clasped.

My first thought was to interrupt her prayers, but I decided instead to sit down a few pews back and wait until she was ready to leave.

I cannot be exactly sure how long the two of us remained there in silence, completely separate, watching as various women approached the confessional.

It was also difficult to contemplate what sort of conversation Dula was having with the Being who, according to her, exploded in her soul when she received the host on Sundays.

By the time she left, the hour dictated that the afternoon light should have receded, but since it was late July, the days were still quite long.

There was no hesitation when we met up. The explanations were brief and Dula got into my car calmly and with no sign of discomfort whatsoever.

We did not put on music that afternoon. Dula clearly wanted to talk. She spoke quietly, with no negative judgments or misgivings.

"I went to church to go to confession. It had been a while since I had done so." She quickly added, "I assure you Patricio, there's no better way to recover your equilibrium than to turn your shortcomings over to God."

"It must be wonderful to have so much faith and the ability to trust the way you do."

"The important thing is not to trust, but to get rid of all the inner garbage. The trust comes later. It's like saying to God, 'Please, accept my ruins and make of them architectural wonders.' "

"It can't help but be a relief to explain to another person the things we don't even dare to think about."

"No, Patricio. I have not confided my problems to another person. That doesn't help anything. I have confided in God."

Dula did not look at me, nor I at her. It was as if rather than engaging in a dialogue, we were unraveling those monologues that human beings sometimes feel compelled to launch into the air.

"In any event, it's hard for me to believe the things you call problems could be so serious."

"So you think I'm an innocent. Don't make that mistake, Patricio. I am not innocent. Nobody is. All human being have their hidden dark side." And after a prolonged silence, "Has Gregorio said anything to you?"

"Yes, Gregorio is worried. He says you aren't the same."

Dula turned towards me suddenly.

"I love your son, Patricio. I've always loved him. I hope you believe me."

She was trying hard to be convincing. But I had the impression she was having trouble finding the right formula to convey it to me. Often language refuses to recreate the truth. We run out of words. "To love." It could mean the same thing as "to be in love with." Can "love" express the world of pleasurable sensations that can end up wounding us? And can this form of "loving" convert the pain of absence into the pleasure of "feeling present" for the one who is loved?

No. Dula was not talking about that sort of love. Without really being aware of it, Dula was talking to me about love-friendship, love-affection. The love one feels towards a child or a sick person, or someone who is suffering.

"I don't doubt it, Dula. I am sure you love my son." And then I told her about Gregorio's suspicions. "He has always been unsure of himself. He has never been convinced that his judgment could be correct. Which is why he feels so confused now. Ever since he was little he has always doubted, feared, consulted, investigated. He was always terrified of making a mistake. And worse yet, sometimes he did make mistakes."

"He's making a mistake now. He has it in his head that there is something more than friendship between Rodolfo and me." And before I could say anything, "The fact is, Rodolfo has been a huge help to me."

"Don't worry, Dula. I know very well my son is mistaken. I have spoken with Rodolfo."

And all at once silence, and the dry feeling in your mouth, and the tightness in the chest.

And the huge sackful of things we wanted to say but did not. A thousand times I've thought that the things one never utters—and the explanations that never really explained anything—are what stay with us for the rest of our lives. And now, six years later, I could repeat verbatim every single thing we wanted to say then, but did not.

When we arrived back at the house, Rodolfo Liaño was waiting for me in the study. "The time has come for me to leave, Patricio. It's better for everyone. I will leave Mas Delfín early tomorrow morning. I'll be back once Dula and Gregorio have left."

That night, Liaño did not join us for dinner. With a look of contempt on his face, Gregorio sought me out to inform me that he and Rodolfo had argued.

"I'm sorry, Dad. But if Liaño stays, Dula and I will go."

I tried to calm him down.

"Don't worry, Son. Rodolfo is leaving Mas Delfín tomorrow."

I glanced at Dula. Her head was bowed, her body slumped.

She said nothing. Not even when Gregorio took her somewhat brusquely by the arm and led her upstairs.

❋   ❋   ❋

There were no official goodbyes. Rodolfo Liaño departed the following day, just as he had told me the preceding night, after we had conversed for some time in my study.

It was a calm exchange, with no attempts at obfuscation or phony and erratic examinations. Frankness prevailed. The truth emerged to sterilize countless elements that had only served to preserve the shaky equilibriums now gone awry.

"What will you do now?" Liaño inquired suddenly.

"Do" was not exactly the right word. The crux of the matter now was how to bear it. How to contemplate a Dula who was no longer the same, to know the main reason for the change and feel powerless to help her.

"It is painful to confirm how happiness can collapse overnight because of a stupid folly or a strange obsession, or some trivial thing that ends up seeming immensely important to us," I said to Rodolfo. "Sometimes I'm unable to take the measure of things. I no longer know what is important and what is inconsequential in this life. But I am sure of one thing. No matter how much it hurts me, I will never betray my son."

"There's a lot that could be said about what is important," replied Rodolfo. "It's all relative." And indicating the open sea, he compared it to the inconsequential strip of the bay. Look at the view, Patricio, and tell me what you think is important? The patch of sea that seems little more than a pond, or the enormous pond we call the sea? I'm saying this because when Chronos devours you and the only thing you have left are your memories, this choice will be important to keep the rest of your life from becoming a living hell."

And seeing that I remained lost in thought, "Remember this. The present is always brief. Try to block out everything you are experiencing this summer."

"That's the worst part, Rodolfo. It's hard to erase what does not and cannot exist."

Until then I had never imagined life could boil down to a simple gesture, or a voice, or a look.

"You know perfectly well why Dula clung to me," Rodolfo said suddenly. "It was her way of fleeing the artificial paradise that was developing between the two of you." And taking a deep breath he went on, "Now she's going to be on her own. Please, help her."

Indeed, it was necessary to help her. And to lie. To lie without words. By inventing excuses to avoid encounters, recklessness, urges. But above all, it was necessary to flee the ghost of the truth.

"Sometimes I wonder how it could have happened. I never imagined I could feel for a woman what I feel towards her."

"Don't look for the reason. It is futile to delve into the realm of human responses. It happened and that's all there is to it. Remember the legend of the basilisk? People believed it was a poisonous snake that did not have to bite because it could kill with a glance. Accept it, Patricio. Human beings are also capable of killing with a glance, or a gesture, or a smile."

I asked Rodolfo when he had realized that Dula shared my feelings.

"I really couldn't tell you. I imagined the attraction must be mutual."

Indeed, it had all happened unexpectedly, furtively, even masquerading as indifference.

We went out onto the balcony. From there, the greenhouse was a great glass mausoleum, a repository for the impossible dreams of a world known only to the plants.

"Sometimes when I go in there I am surprised I don't come across plant skulls," I told Liaño jokingly. In fact, being in love must be very much like feeling rooted in fertile soil and teeming with marvelous blossoms and vegetation. Everything becomes perfume and beauty, but if you neglect the root, it soon dies and the flowers start to emit the most God-awful smell.

Which is why when love cannot be cultivated, when it can never be considered truly ours, the best thing to do is *neglect* it from the outset. Make sure our care does not lead it to believe it could ever be eternal love. In essence, transform dangerous sensations into myths.

There was no other way out. It was necessary to flee Dula and to hope that Dula also fled from me.

"You'll have to redouble your efforts, Patricio," Liaño told me. "In a few hours I'll be leaving this house and I won't be back until they are gone."

That night, neither Liaño nor I slept. It was a light-filled night because the transition from July to August always brings early dawns and the sun, so anxious to rise that morning, soon began to heat up land and sea.

*　*　*

The strange thing is that, six years after Liaño left Mas Delfín due to a fight with Gregorio, the two of them are behaving as if the whole thing never happened.

As a matter of fact, after Miguel's visit to Spain had been planned, Gregorio had no trouble calling him to keep him apprised of the child's trip.

And the little one is here, already a fixture at Mas Delfín which, save for the normal growth of thickets, trees, and hedges, remains exactly the same as it was that other summer.

In contrast, the boy has changed dramatically in just a short time.

There on that little patch of Costa Brava he has learned so many things and has identified so much with them that he no longer misses his home country or believes snake farms are the most important thing in the world.

He has learned the value of the sea beds and beheld a parade of dolphins when his grandfather took him out to sea in the boat. And he has discovered the brutality of the storms and the fidelity of Brutus, who follows him everywhere he goes.

"Can I take him with me to Brazil?"

"The dog belongs to you, Miguel. You can do whatever you like with him."

The worst part about leaving will be to give up the stories grandfather invents for him every night.

"And who's going to tell me the bad and good stories like you do at bedtime?"

Patricio does not answer. He just stares at him, with his legs firmly planted, arms crossed, and an expression much like the one he puts on when Leticia calls him Mr. Proper.

"I don't want to leave you," the child insists.

"I guess one day I'll just have to take off and go visit you in Brazil."

But this eventuality seems awfully remote to Miguel.

"I want you to go with me when I leave." He says it categorically, urgently, at once imposing and beseeching.

"I will do my best to go with you."

But Patricio doubts very much he will be able to keep that promise. There is too much confusion to clear up, too many silences to fill with explanations, for this hypothetical trip to Brazil to come about.

"In any event, if I can't go to Brazil, you can come back to Spain when you're older and live with me at Mas Delfín."

"And when will I be older?"

"Before you know it," responds Patricio. "For us, time has no other limit than death. It is fired from the shotgun of life and before you can say 'amen,' we go from being children to old people."

But Miguel doesn't understand him. The things his grandfather tells him are always real and magic at the same time. They are not, however, always easy to understand.

Right now, the two of them are out on the terrace. The overcast sky has kept them from going down to the beach. The dusty path they have followed every day for two and a half months is fast becoming a quagmire.

Patricio suddenly recalls Dula's last steps as she came up the path towards the house during the sudden downpour that had inundated the beach.

Her footprints had remained there like etchings determined to last forever. Yet they had lasted only a few days. The rain had soon returned, September being the month of constant showers, and the prints had dissolved leaving nothing behind but the memory of their presence.

"As soon as I learn how to write, I'll send you letters," the child assures him.

"And I will send you books."

Recent ones and also his earlier works. Books written by him that talk about his real mother, about dreams tempered by fear and pain, and about absences that never again became presences.

"From now on, I'm going to have you in mind whenever I write a book, you know that little fellow? It will be hard for me to think up a story that you would not be in, one way or another."

And as he speaks, he squints as if something were irritating his eyes.

"When are they coming to get me?"

"In a week."

That's what time is: implacable. It respects no boundaries or constraints and will not be governed by desires or aspirations. Time only knows how to threaten. It pretends to inspire hope, while all along it is devouring it.

"Your father called me this morning," his grandfather explains to Miguel. "It appears he and Estrella are now settled in São Paolo. They'll be coming for you next Monday."

"How many days until Monday?"

"One week."

A sad week. A week distorted by the impending trip. Something the child cannot explain is already filling him with sadness.

"I will tell Dad I don't want to go."

"Don't do that. It will make him feel bad. Your father loves you very much."

"As much as you do?"

"Even more."

"How do you know that?"

"Because he is your dad. And dads adore their children."

"But my dad doesn't play with me like you do. And he doesn't tell stories or take me to festivals or anything."

"But he works to support you and that is very important."

"You don't work?"

"It's a different kind of work. I don't have a regular schedule. In fact this summer I've been very lazy. But after you leave, I'll go back to writing the book I've been working on."

The child slowly draws near his grandfather, leans against his chest and hides his face in his hands.

"I want you to stay with me until my dad comes to get me."

He has said it in a tiny voice, as if he were ashamed to tell him the truth. But Patricio has heard him. He quickly wraps him in his arms and holds him close so the child will feel safe.

"Don't worry. I won't leave you even for an instant."

And he rocks him like a baby. Without speaking. Without allowing the child to speak. He knows any word or sound could open the floodgate of tears.

Once Miguel has settled down, he explains what will happen the day his father comes to Mas Delfín to take him back to Brazil.

"Some people are coming from British television to interview me. I want you to help me out and appear with me on camera. I'll send you a copy in Brazil and you'll be able to see yourself."

"I'm cold, Grandfather."

And the grandfather wraps the child in his jacket.

"We should go inside," he suggests. "It will be dark soon."

The terrace is already enveloped in shadows. The late summer glow is riddled with dark splotches.

"Don't fall asleep before dinner," he says.

"I'm not hungry."

In vain, Leticia protests and calls him a naughty boy. Miguel, his gaze far away, only cries and whimpers.

"Bad habits, that's all it is," Leticia insists.

But the child, hunched over the kitchen table, hides his face to avoid an argument. Fortunately, his grandfather is there. He kisses him. The child's forehead is burning.

"No Leticia, not bad habits. Miguel is sick."

* * *

Burning up with fever, Miguel is no longer the lively, boisterous boy able to dream up a thousand intrigues to bring the grown-ups to their knees.

Now he is a miserable, silent, and whiny boy who only speaks when he wants water or to entreat his grandfather not to let him go to Brazil.

It has been four days of round-the-clock care, defiant coughs, the smell of eucalyptus, and apprehensive footsteps.

They have been to town to buy medicine, but Miguel has not improved. He does not even smile when his grandfather rubs his head and neck nonstop to make him feel better.

"Does your head hurt, little fellow?"

Everything hurt. His head, his body, his smile. Even the light leaking in through the window, which is open a crack.

"Don't worry, Miguel. I'm not going to leave you even for a minute."

It was a matter of bringing down the fever, soothing his burning skin and placing icepacks on his forehead.

But Miguel does not respond.

"Don't fret, little fellow. Grandfather is going to make you better."

In his semi-conscious state, the child sometimes hears voices murmuring. Hushed voices that could be Liaño or else Leticia trying to convince Doctor Gallardo that childhood illnesses can appear to be very dramatic, but what might be cause for alarm in an adult are usually only minor conditions in children.

"The one who's going to get really sick is you, Doctor. Please get some rest."

But Doctor Gallardo does not listen. Doctor Gallardo has returned to his vocation as a dedicated physician and his only respite lies in making sure that the child is breathing normally.

Three days have transpired. Three whole days of wan light, sick-room smells, and muffled sounds, just to be extra cautious.

Three days watching Brutus drowse at his owner's bedside, his nose dry and a sad expression on his face.

In reality everything at Mas Delfín has been turned upside down since Miguel fell ill.

So this morning when, still dozing at the child's bedside, Doctor Gallardo feels the freshness of a child's lips hovering over his face, he thinks he is dreaming.

"Grandfather."

The child is on his feet beside him smiling broadly, his complexion rosy, his features no longer swollen, and a calm expression on his face.

"Grandfather, wake up."

And Patricio realizes the nightmare is over. Miguel is back to normal because it no longer hurts him to talk and his forehead is not burning up with fever.

"I'm hungry, Grandfather."

"That's just what I've been hoping to hear. Being hungry is part of resuscitation."

"Then resuscitate me please."

"Right away. You can eat whatever you like. I'll tell Leticia to make your breakfast."

No more delirium, no more crisis, no more doubts. No more anxious arguments and alarming possibilities. Miguel is better. Miguel is once again a boy whose clock is ticking accurately, the minute hand propelled by the infallibility of time.

No more whispering words that could hurt, or lights dimmed to protect his vision, or windows pulled shut to protect his lungs from further damage. It was all over.

"A good hot bath and you'll be back to your old self, Miguel."

And indeed, there is Miguel, tossing a rubber bone for Brutus to fetch, or dressing up like a Musketeer to poke Leticia's ample backside, or arguing with Canuto because he keeps insisting the sea is too dangerous for him to go out in September.

Once again, grandfather's stories liven up the quiet hours of his convalescence, as do their interminable discussions about the bravery of the Power Rangers and Beckham's goals.

What Miguel still cannot do is go down to the beach, or out in the boat, or fish, because boring old Canuto insists that September is the month of tornadoes and the sea can become enraged with no warning. "You know what, Miguel? Just like you do when Leticia calls you Mr. Proper." And the waves pitch and toss like wild horses.

But grandfather's company makes up for all of it. "I promise you we won't get bored."

It all has to do with metamorphosing certain realities so that the child becomes so immersed in his fantasies he forgets that only three days remain before his father will arrive to take him to Brazil.

Sometimes, when Patricio feels disheartened, he confides in Rodolfo.

"It's going to be rough to see the child leave Mas Delfín."

Liaño does not answer. He knows very well just how alone his friend is going to feel.

"If only I'd never met him."

But he has not only met him, he has woven him into his life.

"I never imagined a grandson could come to be so dear and so necessary."

"His memory will remain with you."

"But memories do not evolve. I want to watch Miguel grow and change."

Which is why it is so risky to trust in the future. Futures never live up to the past. Basically, when he says goodbye to Miguel it will be just as if the child has died a small death.

"You're right, Patricio. It never goes back to being as it was before."

And it occurs to Patricio that to live means this: you forfeit hope to gain memories. Expand emotions to dilute sensation. And above all, you kill illusions to enrich experience.

"I'll have the certainty of knowing that this Miguel—despite the passing years and the changes brought about by time—will always remain the same in my thoughts."

But underneath it all, Patricio Gallardo is not at all sure this metaphysical conclusion is any comfort.

5

Day to day life fluctuated between two opposing forces: "doing" and "undoing." In other words, stockpiling uncertainties, flouting danger, and convincing ourselves that our integrity would enable us to emerge unscathed.

None of us really believes our weaknesses will actually lead us into the traps we stumble upon along the way. We think our innate sense of duty will trump human attraction.

Therefore, while a truce seemed to be in effect after Liaño's departure, it was ludicrous for us to believe that without him, the waters stirred up by entelechy would calm.

His absence was really just a bump in the road. It offered Gregorio a brief respite, but the problem remained.

Indeed, Rodolfo had served as a sort of proscription, which had covered my son's eyes. Without him there, the question was how to keep Gregorio's suspicions at bay.

There were two months to go before Dula and her husband returned to Thailand. Two long months of constant brushes and pretenses that were becoming increasingly unsustainable. No matter what, however, the important thing was to cheat those sixty interminable days. To act as if the tangled mess of urges within did not exist and the moments that presented themselves day after day—unplanned, never intended or even imagined—were just innocuous occasions as far as the three of us went.

Afterwards yes. Afterwards, when the couple was back in Thailand, there was hope that everything would return to normal, and the nightmare of knowing oneself to be untrue would recede.

Distance is the accomplice *par excellence* of forgetting. I was therefore convinced that as soon as I was away from Dula, the strange attraction that had poisoned us since the beginning of the summer would wane.

Absence is like a small death. The kind of death that barely leaves a mark and ends up decaying in the mind like a tomb. There are so many of such deaths in one's lifetime: getting old, changing one's habits, forgetting to dream, retiring, losing contacts once considered essential. The secret is to not give up, to stay in the struggle. And to shut up. That is the main thing. Not to give in to the temptation to "explain to someone" those miniature deaths strewn along the way.

To speak of them is to blow them out of proportion, give them form, make them into something too present and too vital to be forgotten.

I recall now the feeling of relief I experienced after Liaño's departure. I would wake up each morning with the thought that time was passing and nothing had happened. One more day, I would think. It was like winning a battle.

A short while before, Dula, in an expansive mood, had said something to Gregorio during dinner that no one could refute. It had to do with some article she had read about death. "Dying is the easiest way to turn memory into rubble." And she added, "Decay sets in just as soon as memory can no longer feed itself." It was as if she guessed we would never see each other again after she returned to Thailand.

I can still call to mind exactly what I felt a year later when her involuntary premonition came to pass.

It was June and Gregorio had called early one morning to tell me that the birth of the long-awaited baby was imminent. "I'm sorry you're not here with us, Dad."

One year. One year had transpired since their arrival at Mas Delfín. One year of contained silences and veiled hypocrisies. A year of accumulating moments to fill the vacuum bequeathed to us by absence. A year free of barriers, because absence is capable of supplying all the barriers in the world. A year of time frozen into "instants," memories engraved in the air like ethereal snapshots.

Despite everything, nothing could be forgotten.

I'd had to cast about for excuses so my son would not think it strange that my trip to Thailand for the birth of my grandson had not worked out. Gregorio could not understand it. "How is it possible that you are unable to arrange things in order to spend a few days with us?"

I had to employ all of my wits to appear natural. "I have some unavoidable commitments. But don't worry, Son. As soon as I can, I'll carve out a space in my agenda and fly over to Bangkok to meet my grandson." It was vital to sound convincing.

I did not even speak to Dula. It was better to postpone any possible conversation until after the child was born and I, officially consigned to old manhood, could address her like any father-in-law thanking his son's wife for making him a grandfather.

It was also important to be able to keep up communication with my son, free of any shadow of reproach. "Trust, Gregorio. Everything is going to be fine."

No one doubted it. Despite her fragile appearance, Dula was a healthy woman. One of those solid creatures who had no trouble scaling the Daní mountain and swam effortlessly across the bay surrounding Mas Delfín.

Besides, except for the signs of depression that summer, Dula had always exhibited tremendous vitality. She had an energy that infected everyone around her.

I still have not forgotten her comment when the newspapers reported a disease affecting the citrus crop in Levante. "I wouldn't want to turn into one of those lemons infected by the sadness virus." And Gregorio had jokingly retorted that that would be impossible. "Anyway, you would probably turn into a campanilla vine."

And when he saw her so down, so unable to articulate the cause of her depression. "I can't stand to see your leaves blacken and your branches slowly wasting away. Don't let sadness overcome you as it has those citrus fruits."

He said it half-teasingly, but he knew Dula was wasting away inside.

"I'll call you as soon as the baby is here, Dad."

"Please do. I'll stay close by the telephone."

It was a long day. A day completely out of whack. I tried to write but could not. It was no use to justify my nonexistent reasons for avoiding the trip to Thailand. I was nothing but a heap of loneliness and sorrow.

At first, before I knew Dula and Gregorio were expecting, there was still a sense of hope-filled resignation in me. It was hard to explain. I reasoned that a couple without children was like a dead tree which, in the natural world, would culminate in a stroke of lightning. But a couple with children is much more than a dead tree. So when I found out Gregorio was going to be a father, I promised myself I would never see Dula again.

It was no longer a dead trunk. It was a vigorous tree with shoots, branches and leaves and I was nothing more than an intruder capable of destroying the lives of three beloved human beings.

I decided I would forget. Sometimes forgetting is not as a difficult as it might seem judging from the initial pangs. I had Paula. I had the interminable parade of public events to stroke my literary vanity.

And most of all, I had Rodolfo Liaño, the friend who never mentioned Dula to me any more. He too understood that the most effective way to destroy whatever is poisoning us is to drown it in silence.

That afternoon, Paula arrived just after Gregorio had hung up. It's as if I'm seeing her: a glass of whiskey in her hand, her long legs draped across the sofa, and her newly washed hair falling loose around her shoulders.

"Rodolfo told me you're about to become a grandfather."

"It would seem so."

It was a dreary afternoon, but one steeped in feelings, nostalgias, and regrets.

Although she is not an intelligent woman, Paula is good at working the complex web of sensations. And as I have said, she is intuitive. Despite her chronic lack of tact, she definitely knows how to apply her intuition to matters of the senses.

So what was a dreary afternoon to me became a glowing interlude to her.

It wasn't all that difficult. It was a matter of letting oneself be carried away by the flow of alcohol, avoiding conversation, and floating among vague impressions that sometimes impersonate an artificial spark of excitement. Aimless reactions—somewhat empty perhaps or else a bit too bureaucratic—but enough so that afterward a self-satisfied Paula managed to come out with such stale commentary as, for example, "it was wonderful wasn't it, darling?"

That time I really was on the verge of rudeness. I could not stand her kitschy way of using a word like "darling" or posing such idiotic questions concerning an act commonly practiced by any animal in rut.

"You told me you loved me, remember? That's the first time you ever said it."

I turned and looked her straight in the eyes.

"Let me give you some advice, Paula. Never believe anything a man says when he's screwing you."

Paula shrugs.

"No matter what you say or don't say, I know you need me, Patricio. And for me, that's enough to keep going."

Paula was right about that. I did need her. In the same way that I needed my books to be safe deposit boxes for my stifled memories and hidden sorrows, more than literary successes. That is what really lay buried in my intellectual creations.

"We'll have to celebrate the birth, this very night," said Paula.

"Naturally. As soon as Gregorio calls me."

❈ ❈ ❈

When events I am looking forward to are particularly intense, I usually set aside some reserves so as to avoid becoming overly emotional when the moment actually arrives. It does not matter if the event in question has not even occurred yet. The important thing is to be prepared when it does.

Or so I thought when I answered the telephone. But I could never have anticipated that all the things one has mentally rehearsed with such clarity could come tumbling down in an instant.

It is as if a mirror reflecting an actual scene in progress explodes and the scene captured therein remains shattered in the shards of glass.

I don't know why, but I am certain alarm bells went off inside me as soon as I heard the first ring. When I picked up the receiver, I heard the voice of a middle-aged woman.

"Doctor Gallardo?"

"Who is calling?"

"I am calling from Bangkok."

Her Spanish was flawless, but as she began to explain, I had the impression she was speaking in another language.

"Please, who is this? What are you telling me? I don't understand you."

And the truth was, I did not want to understand her. Something inside me was refusing to comprehend what she was saying.

"I am sorry, Doctor Gallardo. I am a family friend. Your son has asked me to give you the news. He cannot speak with you. He is shattered."

It did not make any sense. Not the woman's voice, or Paula's idiotic expression, or the tossing of the trees I was staring at from the balcony.

It was all a huge lie. Even I was nothing but a huge lie at that moment. An irrational being who refused to be a person.

"No one could have anticipated what happened, Doctor. It's been a terrible shock."

But I was still standing there, clutching the receiver, trying to take it in, refusing to accept that what she was telling me was true.

"They're saying it was the anesthesia."

Anything can circumvent fate, ruin plans, and overcome what is apparently invincible.

"Fortunately, the baby boy is fine."

The baby boy. I had not even remembered that the reason for

the phone call—and for the painful explosion of anguish—was the birth of the child.

"Can you hear me, Doctor? I said the newborn is fine."

No. Right then, Miguel did not count. The only thing that counted was Gregorio's sorrow, and the other sorrow that never had the right to see the light of day.

"Please, I want to speak with my son."

It was overpowering. I had to talk to him, suffer with him, despair with him.

"It would be better to wait until he is calmer, Doctor. Your son is going through a terrible tragedy."

It was unimaginable. Nothing fit. Not even the voice talking to me seemed real.

I cannot remember how long I stood there with the receiver in my hand. What really sticks in my mind is Paula's expression as she stared at me wide-eyed, her mouth quivering.

This is what death was like. A bolt rendered inaccessible by a missing key. An impenetrable place where I could never go. A farewell to memories, and to fears of the future, and to the remote and broken dreams of an uncertain future.

"I have to hang up, Doctor. I'll have your son call you as soon as he is able."

Night was falling and shadows engulfed my study.

Paula came over to embrace me.

"Oh my God, what a terrible misfortune."

I told her to leave.

"I would like to be alone, Paula."

She did not want to go, could not understand my attitude.

"I would prefer it if you would just leave."

And she left, trailing my grief behind her.

"As you wish, Patricio."

I went out onto the balcony. I gazed at the sea, the greenhouse, the terrace where we used to gather every evening. And I could hear Dula's voice dissolving into foam on the water, and I smelled once again her violet perfume.

I started talking to her as if she were with me, just as I had done a thousand times before when she could not have heard. "Maybe now you can hear me, Dula. Maybe now you know everything I tried to suppress all summer long. Maybe you can even retrieve the things I used to imagine saying to you when I was alone. Maybe from that other world it will be easier for us to communicate than it was when you were alive. Maybe that's what abundance means, Dula: to hear what we could never hear before, to understand what our ears never heard, and to comprehend what once seemed incomprehensible to us."

I'm not sure how long I stood on the balcony of my study. The night fell suddenly on what had been a stifling day. But I continued talking to her just as if she were there beside me. To die was not just to vanish from the face of the earth. Maybe it was also a form of giving life to those among the living who feel as if they are dead.

And maybe it also meant rest. According to Dula, to die was to be born again into restfulness. I envied her then. She was finally free of the fatigue I felt as I examined our obfuscations, our emotions, and our countless human duplicities.

※　※　※

The loss brought Gregorio and me closer together than ever. The distance was irrelevant. What mattered was our constant desire to be in touch and to share the void Dula had left behind.

At first, our conversations were interspersed with the emotions my son could not suppress whenever he spoke of her. Sometimes he would let me try to cheer him up, as if the wrenching feeling inside him was not inside me as well.

"You're very young, Gregorio. You have your whole life ahead of you."

Initially, however, he couldn't even imagine his life without Dula by his side. "It's going to be like what happened to you, Dad. I'll never find another woman like her."

At the time, Gregorio was convinced no one could ever replace Dula.

Four months went by in this way. Four months of engaging every possible issue and inventing motives to ensure our communication would never wear out or become a mere reflex. It was a matter of stockpiling justifications so that each call was vested with an underlying reason capable of sustaining interest.

Gregorio often talked about Miguel. "You should see him, Dad. He is the spitting image of his mother."

Fortunately, Gregorio's in-laws had taken over the child's care and he was able to pursue his career without having to worry about Miguel. "Even so, it's hard being at the Pasteur Institute without her. She was a brilliant scientist, Dad. I'm lost without her collaboration."

It had been a month, however, since Gregorio had last mentioned Dula. It was hard to decipher the unusual silence. And yet
Gregorio was still affectionate and even seemed to experience
sudden spurts of contentment or joy. "I went to see my son, Dad.
He's adorable."

Then he told me about the Bangkok dancers, the Embassy parties,
new people he had met.

Until one day he confided the truth to me. "I've decided to remarry." He said it out of the blue, with the single-minded resolve
of the indecisive: half-proud, half-terrified.

Then he told me his fiancée's name was Estrella. She was Spanish,
but she lived in Bangkok because her father was a diplomat. "I know
she'll be a good mother to Miguel."

It was like a physical blow. It was impossible for me to accept
that Dula could have been thrust aside so quickly. But I pretended
to be delighted. I congratulated him and tried to hide my disap-
proval. "If Estrella can make you happy Gregorio, then go ahead
and marry her."

I did not for a minute confront him or show him how much his
abrupt desertion had upset me.

Rodolfo Liaño appeared unfazed when I told him about it.

"He's young, he's on his own, and he needs someone to help him
with his son."

But I was not persuaded.

"Dula was irreplaceable, Rodolfo," I said. "I can't comprehend
how he could have put her out of his mind so quickly. She didn't
deserve that."

Once again, I did not go to Bangkok for the wedding. I did, however,
have a chance to talk with Estrella by telephone before the ceremony.
By all appearances, it was going to be a simple event, without too
many trappings. "Estrella has very few relatives. We decided to have
a small, intimate ceremony so as not to upset Dula's parents.

As soon as I heard Estrella's voice, my first impression placed her
squarely in the category of nice people. Her voice was clear, somewhat
lilting, but also serene. "Unfortunately, I'm not a doctor like Dula
was, but I will do everything I can to help your son."

As a matter of fact, Estrella struck me right away as a discerning
and intelligent woman.

And, in effect, she was.

For two years, whenever Gregorio and I spoke by telephone, she
would make an effort to join in. "I've read your latest book, Patricio.

You are a great writer." And she would launch into a discussion of various passages with an expert's attention to detail.

She nearly always told me stories about my grandson. "He's just like his father. He's fascinated by ophidians, lizards, and anything else that slithers along the ground," she teased.

As for Gregorio, he was clearly happy again, as if the whole chapter with Dula had never happened. As if his life had begun with his marriage to Estrella. "All the Spaniards here know you, Dad. You're a very well read author," he'd say. But he took every opportunity to talk about his new wife. "Miguel loves her as if she were his own mother." And he'd add that every day he was even happier he'd married her. "You've asked me what she is like. Well, you've seen the photographs I've sent you. She's tall, blonde, radiant."

I remember when it finally dawned on me that Dula—two years gone by then—had been nothing more than a transitory event in my son's life. I felt as if Gregorio had somehow contributed to her dying. "Dula is really dead now," I told Rodolfo. "No one dies completely until they are forgotten."

That afternoon Rodolfo and I had a long conversation about Gregorio's tension when he imagined that Dula had fallen under Liaño's spell.

"Remember how jealous he was of you?"

"He wasn't jealous, Patricio. It was a symptom of his own insecurity."

Rodolfo was not off base. More than once I had seen that Gregorio was incapable of living up to his wife. He was constantly looking for a way to justify his own sense of disappointment.

"That is why he was suspicious of me. There was no one else at Mas Delfín to suspect."

"But it wasn't until after you left that the real struggle began."

"I know, Patricio. You don't have to tell me that."

❃ ❃ ❃

It was a surreptitious, covert struggle. An apparently insignificant battle that was gradually sabotaging whatever ramparts still remained to buttress our convictions.

The most trifling thing could turn explosive: a casual grazing of the hands, the direction of a glance, an involuntary change in tone, and even the overriding need to flee from our very selves in order not to find ourselves alone together.

It was that fear that compelled me to manipulate Paula shame-lessly for my own ends.

Our relationship was very tenuous at the time and, after the initial infatuation, we had seen each other much less frequently. Still, I did not think twice about pretending her presence was essential to me. I insisted I needed her more with every passing day and that I wanted her by my side constantly, rather than only getting together once in a while as we had been doing since the kids' arrival.

Was I a hypocrite? Of course I was. In principle, all human be-ings are. Even good manners can be symptomatic of an inescapable hypocrisy. Especially when we smile even though we don't mean it, or wash so we don't stink, or acquiesce to avoid an argument, or pretend to ignore the blame of someone who is swearing up and down he did not do it. Make no mistake. Hypocrisy is a deeply rooted human condition.

But Paula was not aware of that. Paula may have been a primitive creature, unpolished, common, and ignorant, but she was also totally natural and devoid of pretense. She was therefore incapable of real-izing that my attentions—particularly after Liaño left Mas Delfín following his altercation with Gregorio—were mainly related to the fact that her presence served as a safeguard against my fears.

"I need you, Paula."

And there she was, puncturing the atmosphere of Mas Delfín with her shrill, strident voice, holding forth about the clients at the Verde Mar hotel or about her girlfriends, or any other drivel that might enter her head. Her absurd monologues were of interest to no one and served only to fill in an ambiguous moment or erase any possible threat from the mind.

I have to acknowledge it. Paula was my main refuge, my wild card, and of course, the most solid excuse I had to justify my constant absences. "I can't have lunch with you today. Paula and I are going into the city."

And so I went about plotting my escapes as the proximity became more urgent with every passing day.

"I probably won't sleep here tonight. Paula wants to spend the night in France."

Gregorio's displeasure was soon in coming.

"Do you realize, Dad, that ever since Liaño left you've hardly spent any time with us at all?"

I glanced at Dula. Her eyes were cast downward and her mouth was trembling almost imperceptibly.

"You're right, Son. It will all be different starting tomorrow."

But the days went by and nothing changed. The essential thing was to pretend, to convey the impression that the only thing on my mind was to be close to Paula.

So I went along sacrificing moments in exchange for hour after hour of tedium. And to make matters worse, Paula was gaining ground. Not for a moment did she suspect that I was using her to fake a level of passion capable of masking my true feelings.

The problem is, as soon as you concede someone a certain status it is tantamount to granting them actual entitlements, and these Paula amassed as if she actually deserved them. It did not even bother her that I never directed a word her way when we were alone together. It was enough to be with me. It was the only thing that really mattered to her.

Even so, something happened that very nearly sabotaged all of the efforts I had been making for two months. There is a chink in every deception that can expose our true intentions.

I've often thought that human mediocrity is far more capable of detecting weakness than those with a reputation for malicious intentions or for never missing a thing. A little jealousy suffices, or a premonition that the terrain sown with such care could be ruined by unexpected circumstances.

As I recall, that afternoon she had decided to cut some flowers in the greenhouse to decorate the house. Although Paula always gave the appearance of being exceedingly compliant, she had taken it in her head once again—and contrary to what Dula and Juliana had always insisted—that flowers were meant to occupy vases and fill empty spaces in order to improve the appearance of the home.

And, although I had expressly prohibited her from yanking the flowers from their beds, she did not hesitate to disobey me and impose her will, buoyed by the very sense of entitlement I had cultivated in her.

I observed her from my study as she entered the building with a pair of scissors and a large, empty basket.

Dula and Gregorio were in town for the afternoon. At least I thought they were. The couple would soon be returning to Thailand and had readily accepted an invitation from friends who wished to say goodbye to them.

I still am not sure why I did it, but the truth is, seeing Paula about to cut the flowers filled me with an uncontrollable defiance. I ran down the stairs and headed towards the greenhouse in a rage.

Just before I went in, however, I discovered Dula behind the structure, leaning against the railing and staring out to sea.

"What are you doing, Dula?"

At first I thought she had not heard me. She seemed lost in thought, focused on the sea as it slowly darkened in the advancing afternoon.

"I didn't expect to find you here. I thought you were in town," I persisted.

She turned towards me with a trace of a smile.

"I thought you were in your study."

"I was."

We were silent for a couple of seconds. Absolutely still. Unable to avert our gazes.

"I wanted to say goodbye to the sea," she explained suddenly.

Her voice was hesitant, cowed, as if she were afraid her words might wound me.

I nodded in silence. It was hard to find the right thing to say. When your surroundings cease to exist and the only thing that counts is the person standing before you, everything becomes confused and words lose their meaning.

"And Gregorio? Where is Gregorio?"

"He went into town without me. I was a little tired and decided to stay."

"I understand."

And again the forced smile.

"I don't expect he'll be long."

All at once I realized she was trembling.

"Are you chilly?" I asked.

"No, you?"

"No."

"There are only a few days left," she said, as if what really mattered was the last bit of the month that still remained.

"Indeed."

I was about to tell her I was going to miss her. But I did not. Besides, it wasn't necessary. Dula was perfectly well aware that I had been missing her all summer.

"Maybe you'll come to Thailand someday."

"It's possible," I replied.

And after a prolonged silence, she turned towards the esplanade and indicated the woods.

"It will be hard to forget Mas Delfín."

Everything was going to be hard. To know she needed that bit of coastline as much as I needed her. Not to be able to contemplate her body as she wades into the sea, or see her descend the path leading to the beach or curl up at Gregorio's feet when we would go out on the terrace to talk after dinner. But most of all, not to breathe in her scent. The unmistakable scent of violets.

Nothing more was said and of course neither of us let on what we were really thinking. Sometimes, however, you can reveal yourself without saying anything at all. The danger can surface when you least expect it and no matter how hard you try to avoid it.

That time the danger was Paula. The ever ignored and manipulated Paula. To tell the truth, I had forgotten she was there in the greenhouse, cutting the prohibited flowers and watching us through the glass.

She appeared at the entrance unexpectedly, scissors in hand and the basket filled with roses resting on a bunch of ferns. She regarded us in silence, as if struck suddenly dumb by the exchange she had just heard.

And that's when I realized that instinct is frequently sharper than intellect, and that the poison of the ophidians can be transmitted to flowers too.

* * *

The worst part was making our way back to the house. The three of us walked in silence, submersed in the unpleasant sensation associated with being caught in the act.

It did not matter that not even the slightest impropriety had occurred between Dula and me. Suspicions are based on doubts, not proof. Proof has more resources at its disposal and is usually susceptible to smoke and mirrors. But the same is not true of doubts, particularly doubts born of intuition.

There is nothing more subtle and straightforward than the inability to reason. No matter how hard we try to discern the truth through reason, it inevitably slips away. Reason can always find an excuse to cover our mistakes.

The storm hit when we got to my study. It is as if I'm seeing Paula toss the basket of freshly cut flowers on the sofa with contempt.

"What? Aren't you going to scold me for cutting your precious relics?"

Paula was defying me for the first time. She was convinced my silence was a way of buying hers.

"So I've caught you red-handed," she said.

"I don't know what you're talking about."

"You're not going to try to deceive me, Patricio. It isn't in your best interest. It would be much too dangerous for you."

I suddenly changed my approach. I became belligerent.

"And just what danger are you referring to?"

And for the first time in her life, she held her ground.

"Don't get angry, Doctor. Now I understand a lot of things. All I had to do was see how you looked at her, and she at you, to get it."

I don't know what passed through my body. It was like an electric current or a blade splitting me into two.

I went up to Paula and covered her mouth with my hand. My eyes bored into hers. And then I clasped her to me hard as if I wanted to break, rather than hug, her.

Then I looked at her again, my horror at the thought of what she might say disguised as a passion I did not feel. Then the rage, and the self-revulsion, and the need for that obtuse mind of hers to absorb what I was about to implant in it as if it were the truth.

"Remember what I am about to tell you, Paula. I can put up with a lot from you because I need you, because I can't do without you. Your lack of experience, your inability to think, your constant rashness, your absolute inability to be tactful. I can even forgive your foolishness. But I will never tolerate your acting jealous, much less when your jealousy is based on something as ridiculous as what you just said."

The crying scene quickly followed. Tears come easily to women like Paula. Then she asked me to forgive her. She said she was stupid, idiotic, anything that might sound self-deprecating. She begged me to forget what she had just thrown in my face.

And I tried to prove to her that all was forgotten. I did it convincingly, so she would believe me. Indeed, the charade was necessary so she too would forget.

I think I succeeded. She never mentioned her misgivings about Dula again. Not even after the kids returned to Thailand and I went back to my usual contemptuous behavior that basically defined our relationship.

In any case, it was not easy. It is never easy to make love out of fear.

❈   ❈   ❈

It has been a tumultuous morning for several reasons.

First there is an over-excited Brutus, recklessly trampling everything in his path, then racing into the kitchen where Miguel is having breakfast, trying to stir up the child, pawing his pants leg and whimpering.

The fact is, Brutus intuits that something momentous is happening. He seems to sense that if he is separated from his owner, he probably will never see him again.

But Miguel does not know what Brutus knows. Human beings are incapable of guessing what certain animals know all along. The only thing he is sure of is that his Dad will arrive at Mas Delfín in a few hours to take him to Brazil, where his mother is waiting for him. But he still trusts his grandfather will go with him.

"Dad won't let you stay here alone."

Not wanting to disappoint him, Patricio nods smiling.

"Anyway, if I don't go with you today, you can be sure I will visit Brazil very soon."

And the child continues eating his breakfast with the ease of simple days, days of light-filled hours, agreeable sounds and enjoyable activities. Miguel is happy. He is not bothered in the least by Brutus' restlessness or Leticia's distressed expression.

As if that weren't enough, Gregorio's arrival coincides with that of the television reporters sent from London to interview him. "They are from Granada TV," Liaño had told Patricio a week ago now, before anyone realized that Gregorio was planning to arrive the same day. "It seems your latest book is quite popular in England."

A number of things are disrupting the peace of Mas Delfín. Even Canuto has roused himself to make sure "the TV people" find everything in its place, tidy, orderly, and above criticism.

"Especially the greenhouse," Leticia had suggested. "The English are very fond of flowers."

But Canuto has anticipated just such a contingency. He spent the previous afternoon cleaning the window glass and replacing light bulbs, restoring to the building some of the splendor Juliana had impressed on it from the moment she decided to build a house for the flowers.

Besides the unfamiliar commotion in the air at Mas Delfín, there is Paula's attitude. For days now she has been declaring to Patricio that their relationship is taking a decidedly unsatisfactory turn, yet

Patricio still attributes her complaints to the hysterical outbursts of a moody female with an excessive need for attention.

Six years of togetherness—even though theirs is a conventional and tenuous relationship, one not given to displays of sentimentality—give him the right to decide whether he should or should not pay attention to his partner's reactions.

So when Liaño tells Patricio that Paula is beginning to tire of her slavery, her submission, and the total lack of attention from Doctor Gallardo, he does not take the warning very seriously.

"You're wrong again, Rodolfo. Women like Paula only pretend to be upset, but they are incapable of changing their habits. One turn of the screw and everything is back in place again." And seeing Rodolfo's disbelieving look, he added, "The most important thing to them is routine. To break off our relationship now would be an irreparable error on her part. Don't forget that, her magnificent appearance aside, her head is empty. Only at my side can she sustain the image of a fascinating woman that gives her such satisfaction. In a manner of speaking, I am her guarantee."

Ever since he woke up, however, Patricio has had the feeling that Liaño's warning was not merely abstract but may have been rooted in some reality.

He has begun to grasp this when, after having tried to reach her by telephone several times without success, she suddenly shows up at Mas Delfín in the midst of all the preparations for the arrival of Gregorio and the reporters from London.

"I suppose you think it's odd that I'm here."

"Absolutely. I've been trying to call you for days."

"I don't spend my time just waiting by the telephone, Patricio."

She's said it with a distracted air, as if "not waiting by the telephone" is the most normal thing in the world to her.

"Well, the important thing is you're here now."

"I'm here because Rodolfo asked me to come. It seems you need me to pose beside you when the TV people arrive."

Patricio now recalls Liaño telling him the night before that he was planning to contact Paula.

"It's good for you to be seen together. You might not think so, but people really do believe that Paula is your muse."

"She could spoil the whole thing," he had responded. "When she opens her mouth, it's goodbye attractive, goodbye beautiful. All she does is repeat cliché after cliché."

But Liaño did not agree.

"It doesn't matter. Paula has charisma. It would be good to have her there."

Patricio tried in vain to convince Liaño that charisma was not enough. When you got right down to it, charismatic types were always less important. They were just people who wore masks to cover up their misery. The essential thing was not charisma but brains, coherence, method, judgment, talent, and clear-sighted integrity. Liaño didn't give an inch.

"Nonetheless, Paula dazzles the public. She even dazzled you when you first met her. Remember? Anyway, she doesn't have to make a speech. All she has to do is smile and be able to say a little something about four pre-rehearsed subjects. I assure you she will enhance your image." And as Patricio showed signs of not believing him. "I advise you not to rely too much on your own opinion, Patricio. No matter how clueless they may be, women have their limits. They also know how to distinguish between a man who is important because of his work, and one who is important because of his sensitivity. And to tell you the truth, your sensitivity has been conspicuous by its absence when it comes to Paula."

"You're not saying that Paula has any intention of leaving me at this stage of the game."

"I have no idea what her intentions are. But when it comes to men, I can guarantee there is more than one out there who would like to persuade her to leave you. Not all men are like you."

And now Paula is there on the terrace, with her unvarying rhythms, her scant intellectual resources, her skewed equilibriums, and Patricio tells himself again that Paula does not have it in her to stray from the doctrine of her preferences, no matter how much other men might try to convince her.

He finally decides to sound her out.

"Rodolfo says you are getting tired of me," he springs on her in a jocular tone. "I don't understand why, Paula. You know I need you."

She gazes at him absently.

"No, Patricio. You've never needed me. The only thing you've ever needed is to use me." And she adds, "I've been putting up with your insults for years now."

She does not speak disparagingly. To the contrary, she gives the impression she is reluctant to speak so frankly about a matter that really no longer concerns her.

"It's probably my fault," she continues evenly. "I was very young when I met you, remember? You fascinated me. It seemed to me that no other man in the world could compare to you. I was dazzled by your intellectual air. You were very attractive. I fell, hook, line, and sinker."

"I guess you're trying to tell me you regret everything about our six years together."

"No. I loved you. And when you're in love, you lose all sense of dimension. I wasn't even bothered by your outbursts of bad taste and your overbearing insults. Yes, I know. You never said you loved me. But I didn't care. To me, the most important thing was not what I could inspire in you, but what you inspired in me."

As a matter of fact, not once in six years had Patricio mentioned the word love. Maybe that is why, when she is finished speaking, Paula remains silent for several seconds with her eyes closed, as if anticipating the accustomed words. "Take it or leave it Paula. I'm not going to pressure you, and I'm definitely not going to change the way I am."

For once, Patricio is speechless.

"You haven't said it. It's all the same. It is quite possible you can't change, Patricio. But I can."

And turning her back, she leaves him standing by the railing of the terrace, the words stuck in his throat.

There is no doubt about it. It has been a tumultuous morning.

❋   ❋   ❋

Ever since coming to live at Mas Delfín, the first thing I would see every morning were the dark, vertical crags jutting from the center of the bay like natural twin sculptures.

After Liaño's departure, I fell into the habit of talking to those crags. Or maybe it was a way of disguising my tendency to talk to myself when no one was around. "They'll be gone soon."

And then I'd wait for the reply. But that time the reply was ambiguous. "Will you feel free? Will you be able to bear your sentence?" And me again, "I don't know. Maybe my freedom is the sentence."

The fact was, Dula and Gregorio were returning to Thailand and the taxi that was going to take them into the city was at the front door.

I remember when I went down to the dining room for breakfast, Gregorio came over to me, that convulsive grin of his tinged with sadness.

"The time is up, Dad. God knows when we'll see each other again."

"The distance doesn't matter, Son. We'll call like we did before. We'll do whatever it takes to keep in touch."

I remember it was an unpleasant morning. It was the end of September and the October chill to come was apparent in the swaying, increasingly bare trees and the angry waves that came crashing into the bluff.

"Most importantly, Gregorio, don't forget to call me as soon as you get to Bangkok."

And Gregorio nodded with emotion, draping his arm across my back

"I'll never forget the good times we've had together, Dad."

Leticia was also moved.

"The summer went by so quickly," she said sniffling.

And Canuto, "You have to come back again next year."

Dula appeared suddenly. Dark circles ringed her eyes and she looked gaunt.

I can see Rosario counting the bags to make sure nothing would be left behind in some corner of the house.

"Goodbye, Dad," Gregorio said, his eyes moist.

And the hug. A fierce hug to show that what we had between us was an indestructible bond of affection that nothing and no one could destroy.

Then Dula threw herself in my arms. I kissed her cheek and she quickly got into the car, leaving on my skin the scent of violets I have never been able to forget.

And now, even after so many years, the scent comes back to me when I least expect it, as if Dula had not died and is still wandering around Mas Delfín half-shrouded in strange mists.

But she is gone, and the more I try to get her back—summon her image, her form—the more she becomes as transparent as the jellyfish that reach out to sting you, camouflaged by the sea.

In any event, our telephone exchanges resumed once they were back in Bangkok. Gregorio was always there when I called. And the months past as if the subterranean torment that had so afflicted Dula and me had never happened.

Two years went by like that. Two years of sadness and joy. Two years without Dula, but with a new wife called Estrella whose friendly voice never failed to connect with me whenever I called. "If you only knew how anxious I am to meet you. Gregorio has told me so much about you."

And the months were free of bad omens. To the contrary, my son and I became increasingly close and even though certain memories occasionally pricked my conscience, they were quickly dispelled by the love between us.

Until without warning, everything changed.

At first there were just a few irritating little symptoms that did not give any real indication of what was to come. Little twists that could even have seemed normal. "I'm sorry, Patricio, he cannot come to the phone. He is very busy. He says he'll write soon." But Estrella's voice, always so forthright, had not sounded sincere to me.

The truth was, the letters did not arrive and whenever I did succeed in getting him on the phone, the excuse was always the same. "The mail is unreliable." But was really unreliable was his voice. "Is something wrong, Gregorio?" And he would not answer. He would just change the subject. "What's the weather like there in Mas Delfín?" or "Make it quick, Dad, I'm in a hurry."

Often Estrella would be the one to pick up the phone. "I'm sorry Patricio, Gregorio is out right now." And even though she tried to sound cheerful, her voice was stiff. "Don't worry, I'll tell him you called."

But Gregorio never bothered to call back.

Time passed and things became increasingly gloomy, yet there was no way to know what could have caused the abrupt change.

"I can't understand what's wrong with Gregorio. He hasn't seemed himself for some time now," I told Liaño on one occasion.

And once again, Rodolfo's silence, and his way of looking at the floor as he always did when he did not wish to come straight out with the truth.

"I'm not making this up, Rodolfo, I can assure you of that. Something is going on with my son. Something I'm not getting. But the fact is, Gregorio is avoiding me."

And Rodolfo abruptly brought up the flowers in the greenhouse.

"If they can breathe and feel, they can probably speak."

The metaphor infuriated me.

That night I called Bangkok again. I found what Rodolfo was suggesting too painful to just leave it at that.

It was better to talk to my son. Ask him straight out what was bothering him. Put doubt to rest, face reality, clear the air. And convince myself that the flowers could not speak. Flowers died, but they did not speak. But Rodolfo persisted, "If it wasn't them, who could it have been?" I finally picked up the telephone.

"Doctor Gallardo?"

The Thai maid could hardly get a word out in Spanish.

"Who's calling?"

"I'm Doctor Gallardo's father. Can he come to the phone?"

I could hear him clearly. The Thai maid didn't have to say a thing.

"Tell my father I'm out. I'm not home. I'm not going to waste my time talking to him."

I collapsed on the sofa. Nothing was right. Not the memories, or the sentiments, or the ideas. It was all a mass of painful confusion. My heart was beating rapidly and something was squeezing my throat, compelling me to cry.

No matter how hard I tried, I could not erase my son's voice repeating a thousand times over that he refused to speak with me, couldn't waste his time.

And from that day forward I never tried to contact Gregorio again. Three years went by and the silence was absolute. No occasion was important enough to induce a call. Not Christmas or birthdays, or the childhood of the grandson I had never met.

For a long time I believed I would die without knowing him. But now I believe that when they come for him, I might die of grief if they deny me the opportunity to see him again.

＊　　＊　　＊

The day before Dula and Gregorio were scheduled to return to Bangkok, I woke up thinking, "only twenty-four hours left. But I still had no way of knowing whether that fact would be my liberation or my punishment.

Gregorio had told me the night before that he and Dula would be going into town the next day to order a few things they would have to pick up on their way to the airport.

Even so, when I woke and went out onto the balcony, there was Dula, under the large umbrella that covered the table where Leticia had served breakfast.

Dula quickly spied me and waved good morning as naturally as always.

I inquired after my son.

She said Gregorio had gone into town alone adding, "I've stayed behind to pack."

Fortunately, I thought, there's Paula. Paula was my ace in the hole to ensure that I would emerge victorious in my struggle to keep my distance from Dula.

The thought of Paula beside me—especially after her major fit of jealousy—dispelled all my fears of falling into perfidy. Paula was not only my ace in the hole, however. In the worst case scenario, she could become my worst enemy. "Hell hath no fury like a woman scorned," Rodolfo Liaño liked to say.

I'd thrown her off the track for the moment. The rest was a matter of time. And to my good fortune, the time was nearly up.

"Have you had breakfast yet?" asked Dula from the terrace.

"No, I haven't."

"Sorry." And taking a last sip from her mug, "I can't wait for you. I've got a lot to do." And without waiting for a reply, she rose and went into the house.

A matter of time . . . It really was just a matter of time. And of Paula. All she had to do was show up, as she had every day that month, and the danger would recede.

Of no consequence now was how tedious I found her company or my irritation at her shrill voice. Paula was my prop, my strength. Without her, it could all come tumbling down.

What no one could have anticipated was that in spite of herself, Paula would contribute to my downfall.

It all began when they called me from the Verde Mar hotel to say that Miss Paula Civanco had taken ill and could I please pay her a visit because she did not want any other doctor to see her. "She has a very high fever, Doctor."

I was not surprised. The night before, she had been gallivanting about the terraces of the hotel clad in her usual low-cut blouses and completely oblivious to the fact that September can be treacherous. It was a month designed to put an end to the excesses of summer, its clouds barely warmed by cold suns and damp nocturnal frosts.

I must confess that under other circumstances, Paula's illness would have been annoying more than anything else. Ever since I left my medical career to write, my devotion to my patients—frequently extolled by Juliana—had diminished considerably.

That day, however, Paula's illness was like a liberation.

I was with her until very late. And when I left Mas Delfín I didn't even have the opportunity to say goodbye to Dula.

"Tell her I will not be able to have lunch with her," I instructed Leticia. "Miss Paula is ill and I will be at the Verde Mar hotel all day."

Leticia could not comprehend my flight.

"You're going to leave her alone? Do you realize, Doctor, that neither she nor Gregorio will be here after tomorrow?"

I did not reply. I got into my car and headed up the hill to get away from the farm as quickly as possible.

Then came the interminable vigil at Paula's bedside. And the obligation to pretend as if her health and well-being were utmost on my mind, and my obsession to fan the flame of our purported bliss at all costs.

It was a rough day, fraught with fear and exhaustion. If a person sets his mind to it, he can turn the appearance of things into a total farce. And that is exactly what I did that day: I set out to deceive. I became the self-sacrificing doctor who thinks only of his patient when in all honesty, I was clinging to her to avoid my own sickness.

And despite it all, two adverse factors came into play: the shortness of the day—it gets dark earlier in September—and Paula's sudden descent into sleep. As soon as I realized she was sleeping I knew my mission was complete and, since it was late, Gregorio would be home by now anyway.

But when I arrived at Mas Delfín, Leticia informed me that my son had not yet returned.

"He called to say not to wait on him for dinner. He's going to be quite late."

Apparently Gregorio had run into difficulties and was going to have to wait until they were resolved.

I asked about Dula. Leticia had no idea where she was.

"After lunch she returned to her room. I guess she's been packing."

I don't know what time it was, nor do I recall how long I remained in my study as the evening wore on.

I remember an overwhelming silence and that my thoughts were becoming distorted, were being poisoned by nostalgia. It was not the rational nostalgia of something long past. My nostalgia was linked exclusively to the future. It was as if my pain had nothing to do with what had already happened, but rather with what could not happen. Until that moment, I had never imagined one could feel nostalgia towards the future and yet, I was experiencing it. It was an imperious force that impelled me, commanded me.

I walked out onto the balcony. Night had fallen. The day has died, I thought. But the truth was, the death quickly turned into an unexpected dawn when I noticed the light on in the greenhouse.

I ran down the stairs and kept running until I reached the building.

I heard music emanating from inside. It was a soft melody, much like the one playing the first time Dula and I had danced together.

I saw her immediately. She was in the middle of the room, beside the furniture Juliana had installed to turn the place into a floral sitting room.

Dula was wearing one of those diaphanous gowns that turned her into a dragonfly and when she saw me she remained motionless, her gaze fixed on mine, her expression calm, as if she had been expecting me.

I walked towards her slowly.

"I've come to say goodbye to the flowers," she said. "I was alone and I guess I needed their company." And, after a brief pause. "I was told that you were away from Mas Delfín all day."

I did not reply. And she went on, "I suppose I should thank you."

"Indeed, Dula. It hasn't been easy. Three months is a long time to struggle."

"I know. I have also been trying to keep away from you."

"It's a relief to know we are now out of danger."

"Thank goodness."

I remember that as she said those words, she inhaled deeply, closed her eyes, and dropped onto the sofa. Then she fixed her gaze on the floor.

"I don't understand what has happened, Patricio. I always thought I knew what I wanted. And suddenly I realize I was wrong. It's all so confusing. Do you think confusion is a form of failure?"

"Failure is the least of it, Dula. What matters are the consequences that can come out of that failure."

She assented without lifting her face.

"We must hold fast to reason," I persisted.

"Yes. I remember you telling me once that reason must be the true 'sensibility' of the writer. I haven't forgotten it, Patricio. In fact, reason must always prevail over our propensities and impulses. Nothing else in this world makes as many mistakes as the heart."

She looked at me again. It was a penetrating gaze, incredibly black. And again her scent. At that moment, the whole greenhouse was a sea of violets.

"It is very clear," she continued, "that no matter how much you think you know someone, he or she will always be a stranger. If we can't control our own sentiments, how can we expect others to do so?"

"Try not to be so hard on yourself, Dula. 'Sentiments' are one thing and 'consent' is quite another. We have not fallen into that trap."

"But my life with Gregorio will never be the same again."

"My life is also changed. I don't think I can ever forget you, Dula."

She stood up again suddenly. She was clearly nervous, as if she were rebelling against something.

"Why? Why did this attraction happen? Do you know the answer to that, Patricio?"

"No I don't, Dula. Sometimes attractions have all the charm of a cobra. But they are there and it is impossible to avoid them."

"Yes, it has been like a poison."

"And yet," I replied, "you once told me that even poisons can cure."

"I remember. Distance can also be a poison. Perhaps it will cure us."

I saw her tremble. I noticed the faint pulsing of the fabric of her dress and the way she pressed her hands together to keep them from floating away.

"Distance and forgetfulness or distance and memory? I'll say it again, Dula, I don't think I'll be able to forget you."

"That's what's so hard, Patricio. Forgetting. Especially forgetting what has never been. My God, Patricio, I love your son. I've told you a thousand times. I've never loved a man the way I love him. What I feel for you is different. It isn't love. Love is self-sacrificing, and I refuse to sacrifice myself for you. But I'm certain that when we part my agony will begin. That isn't love, Patricio. What I feel is a terrible need to be by your side, to hear your voice, to feel your breath, to be involved in your life. Share your problems, your activities, know you need me the way I need you. What should we call that? I don't know: a hex? A spell?

I can still hear the anguish in her voice. And when I thought about it afterward, I told myself Dula probably already knew she was going to die soon. And I understood that if she died, the brevity of always would become the longest never of my life.

And Dula died. She died like the flowers that watched us then from the vantage point of their still vital stems.

But her memory endures. I still have the impression she's alive, that she hasn't gone, is still beside me as she was that evening.

"It would be best if we went back to the house," she said abruptly.

"And then what?"

She shrugged. She tried to smile.

"Then we will have the tranquility of knowing we stood firm."

I assented silently. She tried to joke.

"I wonder what will remain of all of this in a year."

I tried to play along.

"I'll have the staff you gave me when we climbed Daní mountain, and the music of the fountains, and the corner of the terrace where you used to curl yourself up, and of course, the scent of violets."

She lowered her head once more.

"And I? What will I have left, Patricio?"

Her breath was heaving as she asked it, her eyes filled with tears, her body slack, as if she were about to collapse.

I don't know what came over me then. Suddenly everything was moving and unsteady. Everything was divested of its true meaning. Nothing was as it had been just moments before. To tell the truth, I hadn't anticipated Dula's tears, or her becoming suddenly defenseless and despairing.

Which is why I could not answer her. I pulled her to me and held her with all my strength.

Then the silences began. And the fervor rekindled from somewhere deep inside us. And the knowledge that the flowers were watching us with reproach. "Forget the flowers, Dula." We had to forget everything: our consciences, our past struggles. Most of all, we had to forget that when it was over we would never see each other again.

❋   ❋   ❋

As soon as Miguel has finished his breakfast, the reporters from British television begin to arrive.

There they are now, chatting with Liaño, hatching preposterous plans to make the video takes as artistic as possible. They want to make sure the shots of woods, sea, and esplanade can convince the producer that it has been worthwhile to travel all the way to the northeastern coast of Spain to interview Patricio Gallardo, the writer.

Most of them are fair and despite their milky-white skin, they do not stop staring hungrily at the beach in the hopes that once they have discharged their duties, Doctor Gallardo will let them jump into the sea and enjoy the sun, which in their country has not shown its face even once in the past two months.

Then the cables and cameras, and umbrellas to soften the reflected light. And the questions. It's all about questions. How long has Doctor Gallardo been living at Mas Delfín? In what century was the farmhouse built? What are the doctor's favorite hobbies?

And the child. Who is the child? And that extremely attractive woman, what is her name?

142

There are a million things the reporters simply have to know. And discuss. And consult. One does nothing without consulting with Mr. Tarn.

Mr. Tarn is the director of the team. The boss man who, since arriving in Spain, has noticed the dark stains on his temples sliding thickly down his puffy jowls and seen that his rather greasy, shoulder-length hair is clumped with sweat.

"If I could just get a beer, then," he asks.

Leticia does not refuse him. Leticia, while not overly pleased with all the tumult at Mas Delfín, cooperates without a word, because she knows the hospitality shown the newly arrived visitors could have a significant impact on the doctor's reputation.

Miguel also feels a little put out. It seems to him as if a flood of unexpected and heretofore unimaginable things are sweeping away the everyday calm.

Even grandfather seems to be someone else's grandfather. All of a sudden he is dressed in a white linen suit that has nothing whatsoever to do with his everyday attire.

"Why are you wearing that suit?"

"Mr. Tarn asked me to wear it."

Mr. Tarn seems young, because his face is smooth, but he is even plumper than Leticia and besides, when he looks at the boy, it is with a condescending expression, as if he were looking at a monkey instead of a child.

"I hope they leave soon," Miguel tells his grandfather.

But Patricio Gallardo has the impression his guests are going to stay well into the evening.

"If only they'd chosen a different day," he remarks to Liaño.

Worst of all, the commotion is going to ruin his visit with Gregorio. He had hoped his son's arrival would not be stressful. He wanted them to have some time to explain, to understand once and for all why Gregorio had shown such hostility towards his father for such a very long time.

"When Gregorio gets here he's going to find Mas Delfín in an uproar."

Indeed, nothing on that piece of terrain is as it was. Everything has changed. Light and shadows, echoes and voices, human emanations and odors. Here and there, the nose is assailed with the suspicious odor of unwashed underarms and cigarettes.

Even Liaño has changed. Ever since he got up this morning, he has given the impression of one who has a whole host of verbal retorts stuck in his craw that he dare not utter.

"They'll all have to be fed."

"I've already given Leticia her instructions. Rosario is helping her."

Canuto is also helping. Especially when Brutus—always willing to confound an already problematic situation or exacerbate a difficult moment with his canine misbehavior—starts to bark and whirl around the blond "Albions" who, animal lovers or not, cannot help but detest the annoying mutt.

"Come on, Brutus, stop pestering everybody," shouts Canuto.

He quickly grabs the dog by the collar and leads him over to his owner, to keep him away from the labyrinth of cables stretched across the terrace. "Please, Miguel. Pay attention to your dog."

But Miguel does not hear him. Miguel has been guessing for awhile now that no good can possibly come of all of this hubbub.

From the moment he woke up, he has been worried about the tautness in grandfather's face. It is an expression he does not like.

"Grandfather."

At this moment, the two of them are leaning against the railing at the end of the bluff near the greenhouse, their backs to the sea.

"Why are you sad, Grandfather?"

Patricio reacts. He does not want to upset the child. He smiles and bends down to lift him up and sit him on the railing.

Now, with the two of them eye to eye, he regards Miguel, stroking his face.

"I'm not sad, little fellow. But I'm sorry to see you go. I'm going to miss you a lot."

The child does not answer. He watches him. And his gaze reflects everything he is feeling but cannot express

In a way, it is this lack of speech that compels Patricio to summon from the past what time could never suppress. Right now it is not only Miguel who is before him. It is enough to look into his eyes to understand that Dula too is telling him goodbye.

"I could stay," the child proposes.

But his grandfather shakes his head.

"Impossible. Your parents are settled in São Paolo and they want you to be there with them."

"But you are going to be lonely."

That other day too, Dula had said much the same thing. "Will you be able to bear the solitude?" But bearing the solitude is the least of it. Sometimes solitude is as necessary as it is unbearable. The dissonant proximity is what really hurts.

144

"You know what, little fellow? Living alone is not the same as being lonely."

But Miguel does not quite get what his grandfather is trying to tell him.

"I'll ask Dad to let me stay with you," he insists.

His mother did not want to leave either. She too had said, "If only I could stay here forever." But Gregorio had taken her. And when she left, everything began to die. Even the flowers in the greenhouse had not been the same.

The only thing that remained alive after their departure was her voice. He almost never missed a chance to hear it when Gregorio called him. "Are you well, Patricio? Everything is fine here. Gregorio and I are doing great." But she would quickly say goodbye. "Take care of yourself. I send you a big hug."

That was the happiest time for Gregorio. Dula had gone back to being herself again, especially when she found out she was expecting.

"We are very happy, Dad, I can tell you that," Gregorio insisted. And he'd launch into the minute details of his private and professional life, which he never failed to share with his father. As always, it was Patricio who cut the conversation short. "Try to be a little briefer, Son. This call is going to cost me a fortune."

But Gregorio's enthusiasm never dimmed. And the calls went on month after month with a vitality that never settled into tedium. Although Dula's voice seemed to be fading. It was gradually wearing out, like the water from the fountain after the drought set in.

"Is something wrong, Dula?"

"No. I'm just a little tired."

And she'd pass the receiver back to her husband so the two of them could continue their conversation.

Until one day her voice was extinguished forever. And it was as if Gregorio's grief was joined to his own. For four months, they felt the need to mention Dula every time they spoke, to describe Dula, to recall her features.

Then Estrella came on the scene and Dula began to recede from Gregorio's memory. He no longer said to his father, "How am I going to go on without her, Dad."

But the communication between them remained constant for the next two years. Two years that sped by, because Patricio had delved into his work and the hours rushed past.

Until the silence.

"The best thing to do when your son gets here is to ask him straight out what happened to make him act so strangely. Certain confidences are best handled face to face," Liaño suggested.

What Patricio finds the most mystifying is that his son has preferred to speak with the person he once considered his rival—rather than with his own father—to discuss the details of Miguel's trip.

He didn't even want Patricio to come to the phone when he announced his imminent arrival.

"Please, Rodolfo. Just tell the 'writer' I'll be there on Monday to pick up Miguel. And make sure everything is ready."

"Don't you want to speak with your father?"

"It isn't necessary."

And he had hung up.

Indeed, everything is ready for the child's departure from Mas Delfín. Leticia has been working since first thing in the morning to make sure nothing is missing from the child's suitcase.

Sometimes Miguel feels pensive when Liaño and grandfather discuss certain topics. He does not understand why something very serious passes between them, especially when they are discussing his father.

One thing for sure is that this morning everything is all in a turmoil, what with the journalists' admonitions, the devices the technicians are handling, and the excruciating noises permeating the air. He is also bothered by Paula's presence. She is pacing about the terrace as if she were one of those models in Leticia's magazines. And the questions those people are asking in their deplorable Spanish.

"Remember, Miguel, if one of those men asks you about Paula, you have to tell them she is your grandfather's muse."

But when Miguel asks Liaño what the word means, Rodolfo gets distracted and leaves him there by the door of the house while Brutus, still barking excitedly, does his part to ratchet up the noise.

Miguel notices his grandfather and Paula listening attentively to Mr. Tarn's instructions. "They'll have to explain where they met and how long they've been together," Liaño explains to the child.

"Why?"

"Because that stuff 'sells.' Then you'll have to say something too. Your grandfather wants you to be there when the cameras are rolling."

"And what do I have to talk about?"

"Whatever you like."

"And what if what I say doesn't sell?"

But Liaño has not heard him. Liaño is too busy and he cannot rely solely on the child.

In any case, something is going on and while it appears to be having no affect on the general atmosphere, it is definitely throwing things out of whack.

Liaño notices when Paula draws near Patricio to tell him she needs to speak with him.

"I'll be very brief, Patricio."

Liaño guesses what she is about to say. Paula has been spending too much time contemplating herself in the mirror and realizing that her looks are what seduce and the years are unforgiving. It stands to reason, then, that if she delays too long in figuring out her life as an adult, she'll end up cast aside with her vanity—malnourished on flattery—and her vocation as a faithful woman, which could easily be trampled by the worst form of infidelity: boredom.

Besides, while she may not be overly intellectual, Paula is shrewd and she knows that there is literary prestige and then again, there is the prestige of wealthy men. Some men would pay a fortune to walk into a room with her, to be able to show her off as a trophy.

This is why she has asked Patricio for five minutes of his time.

"Go ahead. Out with it. What's wrong with you?"

"Wrong? Nothing. I just wanted to tell you something so you could be prepared for the consequences."

She says it without raising her voice, as if she had used all the free time Patricio gave her over the summer to take a class in diction.

"I'm waiting. Go on."

Paula does not even clear her throat. She merely tosses her head to get her hair out of her face.

"I've come to Mas Delfín to help you out. Don't worry. I'm not going to ruin your literary career or do anything that might throw a damper on your writer's egotism."

"I appreciate that."

"But I want you to know that after this final literary travesty, I will never return to Mas Delfín."

Patricio has not fully grasped what Paula is trying to tell him. And the fact is, he couldn't care less either.

"What kind of bee has gotten into your bonnet? You don't like to swim on my beach or join my intellectual circle any more?" he inquires sarcastically.

"That has nothing to do with it, Patricio. I won't be coming back because I'm getting married."

At first he does not believe her. Sometimes Paula says stupid things just to attract attention. Absurdities such as, for example, that she has seen a little green man with antennas on his head walking naked in the woods, or that the Verde Mar hotel is housing a guru who can levitate when he is meditating.

Everybody knows that Paula's fantasies, while hardly convincing, are one of her foibles. And she does occasionally manage to entertain whichever idiot happens to be listening to her at the time.

But this time, what she is telling Patricio rings true.

"So you're getting married. And might one inquire as to who is the lucky gentleman?"

Paula is unruffled.

"You don't know him. He is a foreigner. An American to be exact, from Texas. It seems he's an oil magnate and he is intent on marrying me."

Patricio is somewhat disconcerted. Paula seems to be telling the truth.

"Do you love him?" he asks.

She nods her head and smiles.

"A lot more than I love you right now, and a lot less than I loved you when I met you."

"So you did come to love me. You never told me so."

"I didn't think it was necessary. The important thing is not to say 'I love you,' but to show it. And I think I showed it, with interest." She paused briefly. "I showed it every single time you humiliated me. I never complained."

Patricio averts his gaze and frowns. For a second Paula's look seemed to shoot flames. It is as if her look has somehow penetrated his brain in its desire to burn his conscience and rake his soul over the coals.

He had never examined things from this angle. Had never tried to understand other people's motives or examine the tears that one might cause, or consider that it is not necessary to pay attention to those who bother one, or help those who need one.

"I never explained to you what it was like to find myself relegated to nothing by your intellect and to know that everything I did or did not do was tactless, uncouth, or stupid. But it's all over. I don't love you like I did before. And when it comes down to it, I don't admire you either. Tyranny and indifference hurt. They wear you out and they end up changing how you feel."

Patricio reacts then. He suddenly realizes that Paula is no longer the silly little girl she used to be. Right now, Paula is a small time executioner who could perhaps have been the love of his life had Dula not crossed his path.

"Forgive me, Paula. You are right. I don't deserve you."

And he doesn't even understand that by saying those words, he is hurting her more than if he had actually tried to put up a fight.

✳   ✳   ✳

Gregorio has arrived. He is driving a rental car and, as usual, he has pulled up on to the esplanade before the front door of the house.

But the commotion caused by the reporters and Brutus' barking have muffled the sound of the vehicle, so that when he gets out of the car, the residents of Mas Delfín are just realizing he is there. His torso is a little thicker, the lines on his face slightly more pronounced, and his hair is graying slightly at the temples.

The first to notice him is Leticia. A Leticia six years older but just as effusive. A Leticia whose flesh spills out all over the place as she approaches and whose heavy pants begin deep in her chest.

"There is my boy."

And then Miguel, running behind her and Brutus hot on his heels, wagging his tail and even his ears.

Behind them, Rodolfo quickens his pace and compels Patricio to do the same.

"Come on, hurry up. We have to go meet him."

But Patricio hesitates. Patricio still doesn't know how this son of his is going to react after three years of refusing to speak to him, up until the day he asked him to take care of the child.

He moves towards the vehicle anyway—because to remain on the terrace could make things worse—, Liaño whispering instructions to him all the while.

"Above all, act natural, Patricio. You have to act as if your son's silence does not matter."

But three years of silence are a lot of years. Three years of silence are like three centuries of doubts, of question marks. A litany of hypotheses that lead only to bottomless pits.

It does not matter. In any event, the tension is broken because his father has no sooner descended from the vehicle than Miguel has thrown himself in his arms while Brutus, still totally keyed up, sniffs the newcomer's shoes to determine whether or not he is welcome.

Miguel is happy. Miguel is still hopeful that his father's presence will not interfere with his rapport with his grandfather. To Miguel, the important thing is that both men remain at his side and that the wonderful moments he has experienced over the summer with Patricio are not just a temporary thing, but can be stretched to last his whole lifetime, without his ever having to give up anyone he loves.

Miguel is thinking this because he is ignorant of the duplicity of adults. He cannot conceive of a father and a son who treat each other like strangers. So when Gregorio places him on the ground and turns to face his grandfather, the child does not understand why they just stand there impassively, as if they are hesitant to approach each other.

All they do is stare. And the expression of both men contains only curiosity. They do not even smile. They just survey and assess, and it seems as if they are afraid to touch each other.

"You've aged, Son," his grandfather says.

But this does not seem to bother Gregorio. He nods. The truth is, the Gregorio standing before Patricio is now a mature man, someone who would be hard pressed to say, "Help me out, Dad; do you think I'm making a mistake?" No, Gregorio no longer looks like someone who makes mistakes or hesitates. This Gregorio is a man who is sure of himself, his movements, his actions, and his decisions.

It is clearly reflected in his expression, which is sardonic and cold. He suddenly raises his head and indicates the temporary platform that the team from British television has erected.

"I came on a good day," he remarks. "A little party."

Liaño explains what is going on.

"I am so sorry your visit has coincided with this invasion."

But to Gregorio the invasion is like a breath of fresh air.

"It doesn't matter. I'll be leaving soon."

Leticia protests. She cannot accept that her child has come all the way to Mas Delfín only to take little Miguel and turn around and leave again.

"I've prepared your favorite meal."

"I'm sorry, Leticia. I really don't have much time. I thought I'd warned you to have everything ready when I arrived."

And suddenly Paula appears. Gregorio is watching her on the terrace, steering her magnificent anatomy among the cables, cameras, reporters, and helpers, and the endless array of devices that have turned the scenery into a one big technological wasteland.

"I see Paula hasn't changed," he remarks.

Patricio does not reply. He would like to explain to his son what

Paula has just told him, but he understands that certain explanations are not warranted and might further exacerbate the discomfort of the moment.

"How do you find Miguel?"

"He has grown. He's very tanned."

And at hearing his name mentioned, Miguel jumps in. He eagerly tells his father that grandfather has given him lots of gifts, and taken him to the town festival, and thrown him a birthday party with clowns and lots of kids.

"Dad, I promised Grandfather we would take him to Brazil with us. We can't just leave him here alone."

But Gregorio seems not to hear. Now he is chatting with Canuto and telling Rosario to please bring down the child's suitcase because he is in a hurry.

"The highway is a mess and the traffic jams heading into the city are going to be a nightmare."

It does no good either when Miguel pulls hard on his pants leg to get his attention and insists that if grandfather doesn't go with them, he does not want to leave Mas Delfín. Gregorio does not seem to notice the remark, much less his father's desolation.

Patricio is standing there in silence, his face clouded. He is like a fugitive from himself, motionless and oblivious to everything except the child.

"Do you hear me, Dad? I want grandfather to go with us."

But Gregorio is becoming irritated by the dog's antics.

"Will someone get this mutt away from me," he exclaims, poking Brutus with his toe.

"His name is Brutus and grandfather gave him to me," retorts Miguel, suddenly becoming Mr. Proper.

But Gregorio is not persuaded by this sort of gift.

"You really don't believe the dog is going to Brazil too."

"Why not?"

"Because whims can turn out to be costly and they always turn out badly. There are dogs in São Paolo too."

He has said it harshly, like an ultimatum. And Miguel feels humiliated. His father has never spoken to him in such a despotic way before. Truly the world of grown-ups is a pitiless world, fraught with misunderstandings and always ready to assail you with painful uncertainties, the child is thinking in his own way.

So although no one appears to notice what he is going through, Miguel feels an overwhelming urge to cry. And yet he controls himself by swallowing his saliva and squeezing his lips together so the quivering of his chin is lost in fake sighs.

But his grandfather realizes Miguel's predicament and takes him in his arms.

"Your father is right, Miguel. I will take care of Brutus. I promise I will. And when you come back to Mas Delfín, he will be waiting to play with you."

Sometimes, however, attempts to "comfort" can backfire. Often the consolation offered does nothing more than intensify the sadness, turning it loose and creating a different sort of torment.

So even as his grandfather rocks him, the suppressed sobs burst forth. Miguel is no longer able to control himself. It is impossible to detain what has abruptly destroyed the perfect symmetry of each and every assumption we had made to nourish our hopes and illusions.

What is more, it can't be good when every pleasant prospect is being transformed from one minute to the next into cause for disappointment and disillusion.

"Come on, little fellow, be reasonable."

But at age five, reason is not measured by logic or dictated by common sense. At five, common sense is an unattainable utopia that shoots down dreams and turns life into a battleground.

So Miguel clings to his grandfather, and begs him not to leave him.

"I want to stay with you," he insists. "I don't want to go to Brazil."

For several seconds, a strange silence settles upon them, more piercing even than Miguel's sobs. A silence that upsets rather than calms and is on the verge of sabotaging the veneer of politeness which everyone has managed to sustain up to now.

"That's enough, Miguel," orders his father. "Give your grandfather a kiss and get in the car."

And Miguel gives up. Miguel knows that no matter how much he protests, his father is going to be inflexible on this point and grandfather—even though he would like to persuade his son that his grandson is going to feel a tremendous sense of loss if he does not explain to him nicely why Patricio cannot travel with them—will never succeed in changing his mind.

"Come on, little fellow. Hop in the car," insists his grandfather.

And Miguel obeys, sobbing. There he is now, watching his grandfather from the back seat, his eyes red from crying.

He does not even care that Leticia and Liaño come up to the car window to cheer him up and say goodbye. Miguel does not appreciate the efforts grown-ups make. Miguel is just a small child incapable of gauging the magnitude of all those gestures, sounds, and expressions. He only knows the value of impediments and impositions and, most of all, pain.

"I'm sorry you're leaving so soon," Patricio tells his son as he prepares to get behind the wheel.

The two are alone momentarily. No one can hear what they are saying. The racket in the background, the child's crying, and Brutus' incessant barking, have cut them off from the others.

"In contrast, I am never going to be sorry about that, Dad," replies Gregorio dryly, getting into the car. "There is nothing I want more than to get away from this God-forsaken place and everyone in it."

"My God, what is wrong with you, Gregorio? Where has all this hate come from all of a sudden?"

Gregorio does not look at his father. Clearly nervous, he tries to start the car.

"There's nothing sudden about it, Dad. I've hated you for three years."

Patricio hesitates. He doesn't understand. He is afraid he has misinterpreted what Gregorio has said.

"You said you've hated me for three years? Why?"

"Think about it, Dad. It would be strange if I didn't hate you."

Their eyes meet. They both know that the tension that began to tear them apart three years before is now coming to a head. Ignorance is about to become knowledge.

"I hope to God your children never treat you the way you are treating me now, Gregorio," his father reproaches him in a trembling voice.

But Gregorio does not flinch. He smiles. Then he puts the car into first and moves to start it.

"It's funny you should mention my children," he says, shaking his head. "Don't worry, Dad. It's not likely I'll be having any more children."

The motor groans and the tires begin to move, but Gregorio is not finished.

"To be more precise, I have to admit that Miguel is not even my son. I'm sterile, Dad. I found out three years ago, after Estrella and I had been married for two. The specialists diagnosed it."

Patricio does not react. It is Gregorio who continues.

"Come on now. Don't just stand there so innocently. At first I thought Rodolfo Liaño was to blame, but I was persuaded otherwise when I recalled that Liaño left Mas Delfín nearly a year before Miguel was born."

Patricio closes his eyes, refuses to contemplate his son's expression. To dwell on those cold, hardened eyes, full of hate, would be like plunging into an inferno.

"That's how I figured out it was you. It couldn't be anyone else. So now you know who this grandson of yours is. I hope you remember him well, because you're never going to see him again. At least that is my intention."

"Wait a minute."

"No, Doctor Gallardo. I'm not going to wait. I only want to say to you what I should have said a long time ago. You took Dula away from me, and now I'm going to take your son away from you. That's why I sent him here to Mas Delfín. So you could meet him and know what it's like when your own blood robs you of the most essential part in your life."

And with that, Gregorio steps on the accelerator and speeds up the drive towards the highway.

* * *

The voices multiply and grow thick, filling the air at Mas Delfín with dense sounds that occasionally seem to materialize as some viscous substance.

Patricio's intuition tells him that some of those voices are asking him questions and that he is answering, although he does not have a clue what he is saying. They are stupid questions bogged down in banalities. Questions that invite one to digress or talk around the point. They make the writer out as a puppet without strings, someone devoid of cogent opinions. Everything is coming out hollow words, undecipherable symbols, and clichés in the guise of pleasantries.

But it's all a lie. Thinking is not the same as responding to the stereotypical phrases imposed by the director. Thinking means entering into the void and observing how ideas slither in and out through crevices of confusion and ignorance.

"Please, Doctor Gallardo, remember to speak in English."

And Doctor Gallardo nods. English is the universal language, understood by all. It would be helpful to make sure his accent is correct and his responses leave no doubt as to his power of description.

"Fine. Go on then."

The sentences bunch up and disperse, replete with the same stale topics brought up time and again in all the interviews.

"Does it bother you to live alone?"

"Are you a good Christian?"

Doctor Gallardo hesitates before responding, then clarifies.

"I would have liked to have been."

And he realizes that what he really would have liked was not to have been a good Christian, but to have been a good husband and father.

"The only thing I have managed to do, however, is be a good writer."

And the journalist keeps on asking questions. He persists, slowly and conscientiously, never once deviating from the lines Mr. Tarn has written out for him on a piece of paper.

"How many children do you have, Doctor Gallardo?"

Doctor Gallardo suddenly falls silent. He frowns and regards the journalist warily.

Then he closes his eyes. Sometimes the truth no one is aware of can be blinding, or irritating, might moisten the eyelids.

But Doctor Gallardo takes himself in hand. Looking squarely at the camera, he says evenly, "I had two sons. But I have lost them both."